Unlucky in Love . . .

Steven's mouth went dry, and he felt his face flush with embarrassment. Just as he was holding a sandwich under his chin and waving his other arm around like a lunatic, Jill Hale had to show up!

"Have a seat," Joe Howell said to her. "Steven was just showing me how you are supposed to hold the trombone."

Jill smiled at Steven. "Great. Let me see."

Steven felt silly, but what could he do? "Well, you have to keep a steady grip on the slide," he said. "Then you have to move it like this." He thrust his arm forward, and as he did, he knocked the milk carton off of Joe's lunch tray.

Steven watched in horror as the milk carton flew up, turned over, and landed on Jill. Milk spilled all over the front of her shirt and into her lap, and for an awful moment, Steven felt as if he might even cry.

Bantam Skylark Books in the SWEET VALLEY TWINS AND FRIENDS series.
Ask your bookseller for the books you have missed.

SWEET VALLEY TWINS
AND FRIENDS

Big Brother's in Love!

Written by
Jamie Suzanne

Created by
FRANCINE PASCAL

A BANTAM SKYLARK BOOK
NEW YORK · TORONTO · LONDON · SYDNEY · AUCKLAND

RL 4, 008–012

BIG BROTHER'S IN LOVE!
A Bantam Skylark Book / March 1992

*Sweet Valley High® and Sweet Valley Twins and Friends are
trademarks of Francine Pascal*

Conceived by Francine Pascal

*Produced by Daniel Weiss Associates, Inc.
33 West 17th Street
New York, NY 10011*

Cover art by James Mathewuse

*Skylark Books is a registered trademark of Bantam Books, a division of
Bantam Doubleday Dell Publishing Group, Inc.
Registered in U.S. Patent and Trademark Office and elsewhere.*

ISBN 0-553-15943-7

Published simultaneously in the United States and Canada

*Bantam Books are published by Bantam Books, a division of Bantam
Doubleday Dell Publishing Group, Inc. Its trademark, consisting of
the words "Bantam Books" and the portrayal of a rooster, is Registered
in U.S. Patent and Trademark Office and in other countries. Marca
Registrada. Bantam Books, 666 Fifth Avenue, New York, New York
10103.*

PRINTED IN THE UNITED STATES OF AMERICA

OPM   0 9 8 7 6 5 4 3 2 1

To Kimberly Bloom

One

◇

"I think we'll use these shots," Elizabeth Wakefield said as she spread a collection of photographs across her bed. Elizabeth and her closest friend, Amy Sutton, were working on a story for Sweet Valley Middle School's sixth-grade newspaper. Elizabeth was the editor of *The Sweet Valley Sixers*. "We'll do the story on the gym renovation all in pictures—like a photo essay. That'll be a first for the *Sixers*."

"I always thought I wanted to be a writer someday," Elizabeth continued. "But I'm having so much fun with my new camera, I think maybe I'll be a photojournalist."

"These really look professional," Amy said as she admired her friend's work. "I think you've got talent."

"It helps to have a good camera," Elizabeth said as she put in a new roll of film. "I'm so glad Aunt Helen gave us that money so I could buy it." Elizabeth's great-aunt Helen had recently visited and given each of the Wakefield kids a hundred dollars to spend however they liked. "Let's go downstairs. I promised Jessica I'd take a group picture of the Unicorns. They're having a meeting downstairs."

Jessica was Elizabeth's identical twin sister. Both girls had long blond hair, blue-green eyes, and a dimple in the left cheek. In fact, they looked so much alike that only their family and very best friends could tell them apart.

Amy groaned. "It's not for the paper, is it?"

Elizabeth laughed. The Unicorns were a club made up of the most popular girls in Sweet Valley Middle School, and they liked attention anywhere they could get it. "No, it's just for fun. I thought I'd try my talent on human subjects."

Amy giggled. "Since when are the Unicorns human?"

Elizabeth giggled, too. Neither Amy nor Elizabeth was a member of the Unicorns. Elizabeth had been asked to join the club, but she felt she didn't have much in common with most of the girls in it. While the Unicorns enjoyed talking about boys, clothing, and movie stars, Elizabeth preferred reading a good mystery and spending time with close friends.

Jessica, on the other hand, loved being a member of the Unicorns. But despite their different interests and friends, Jessica and Elizabeth were very close. So when Jessica begged Elizabeth to take a group picture of the Unicorns, Elizabeth had happily agreed—as long as they didn't expect her to put it in the paper.

"You go," Amy said as the two girls went down the stairs. "I think I'll sneak out. I've got a million things to do at home."

Elizabeth could hear the Unicorns talking and laughing in the living room. "OK," she said as Amy slipped out the front door. "I'll see you tomorrow."

"Elizabeth!" Jessica exclaimed when she saw her twin. "Wait until you hear this! Janet has two tickets to *Staying Up with Bob!*"

Elizabeth's eyes opened wide. *Staying Up with Bob* was her favorite show on television. "That's amazing, Janet," Elizabeth said. "It's filmed in Los Angeles, right? I heard those tickets are impossible to get."

"Well, it *was* difficult," Janet admitted. "Let's just say I have connections." Janet Howell was an eighth grader and the president of the Unicorns. Most of the Unicorns thought she was the most important girl at school.

"Who are you going to take with you?" Elizabeth asked.

"We were just discussing that," Janet said. "It's going to be really difficult to decide. It will be a Unicorn, of course. But I haven't quite made up my mind which one."

Elizabeth looked around the room at all the excited faces. Jessica's eyes were shining with hope. For the first time, Elizabeth almost wished she were a Unicorn. She would give anything to see *Staying Up with Bob*.

"Wait a minute, Janet," Lila Fowler whined. "I thought you were taking me. We *are* cousins, after all."

"The show is in three weeks," Janet said, ignoring Lila and addressing the Unicorns authoritatively. "I think that should give me enough time to decide who *really* wants to go."

Elizabeth rolled her eyes. She knew that Janet probably would make the other Unicorns miserable for the next three weeks by asking them to run her errands and perform ridiculous dares.

"I think my trip to *Staying Up with Bob* would

make a good story for the *Sixers*," Janet added. "Don't you, Elizabeth? I'll write it myself and . . . oh, hi, Steven."

Elizabeth turned just in time to catch a glimpse of her fourteen-year-old brother passing through the living room on his way to the kitchen. Steven didn't answer.

"*Hello, Steven*," Janet repeated loudly.

Steven didn't even turn around. He just walked through the room like a zombie.

Elizabeth was not surprised. Steven had been moping around for days. He was so wrapped up in his own thoughts that he no longer even noticed when people were speaking to him.

"Don't take it personally," Elizabeth said quickly. "Steven's just been in a horrible mood lately."

"I can guess why," Janet said with a nasty grin. She turned to the other Unicorns. "He's got a bad case of Jill Hale-itis."

Tamara Chase and Kimberly Haver giggled.

Janet is such a big mouth, Elizabeth said to herself.

"What's Jill Hale-itis?" Belinda Layton asked.

"Jill Hale is this really pretty girl in ninth grade at Sweet Valley High," Janet said importantly. "She has blond hair down to here"—Janet put her hand just below her chin—"and green eyes, and Steven Wakefield is *totally* in love with her."

Elizabeth couldn't really argue with that statement. Steven did have a terrible crush on Jill, and it made him impossible to live with. He had recently taken all the money Aunt Helen had given him and taken Jill on a date to a really fancy restaurant. The date had been a disaster and ever since then Steven had been depressed.

Janet waved her hand dramatically in front of her nose. "And somebody should tell Steven that drenching himself in aftershave isn't going to make Jill pay attention to him—especially since he doesn't even shave."

The Unicorns all laughed hysterically. Elizabeth felt her cheeks grow hot with anger. Maybe Steven *was* acting like an idiot. But Janet didn't have to be so mean. How dare she make fun of Steven? Elizabeth was determined to stand up for her brother. But before she could get the words out of her mouth, she heard the loud, shrill beep of the smoke alarm in the kitchen.

"I can't believe it," Jessica shouted as she raced into the kitchen. "He's done it again."

Elizabeth ran into the kitchen with the Unicorns behind her. Black smoke was seeping out of the oven. Jessica quickly turned the oven off and removed a pan.

With a spatula, she scraped off the charred remains of some slice-and-bake cookies. "That's the fourth time this week that Steven's put something in the oven and forgotten about it," Jessica complained. "Where is he, anyway?"

"Staring into the sunset and dreaming of Jill," Janet said snidely. She pointed toward the windows that overlooked the patio, where Steven was sitting in a deck chair. He was staring off into space with a dazed look on his face.

"Jill Hale has that effect on men," Janet said. "I should know. She's dating my brother, Joe. Get this—last week Joe put on a string tie and a cowboy hat and took Jill square dancing. Any girl that can get Joe to dress up like a cowboy and do-si-do is a real heartbreaker."

"I wish I had that effect on men," Tamara Chase said as she opened a window to let some of the smoke out of the kitchen.

Just then, the phone in the kitchen rang. Elizabeth walked toward it, but before she could pick up the receiver, Steven ran into the kitchen and grabbed it.

"Hello," he said in his deepest voice.

Even Elizabeth had to bite her lip to keep from laughing. She thought that Steven sounded like a sick frog. Then, in his regular voice, she heard Steven say, "No, she's not here right now. This is her son. Can I take a message?"

The Unicorns ran back into the living room and collapsed into giggles. Elizabeth couldn't help laughing too. *Poor Steven,* she thought.

"Steven doesn't really think Jill Hale would be calling *him,* does he?" Janet said when the giggles had subsided. She turned to the others. "First of all, she's going out with my brother. Jessica, you and Elizabeth better be prepared to watch Steven make a complete fool of himself."

"Oh," Jessica said, "Steven's like this all the time. It's not just Jill Hale."

"Jessica!" Elizabeth cried. She knew Steven was *not* like this all the time. She was just about to come to her brother's defense when she felt Jessica poke her in the back.

"I know Jill is pretty and everything," Jessica said. "But by next week, Jill Hale will be history and Steven will be mooning over somebody else. Steven is *very* fickle."

Elizabeth stared at Jessica, completely bewildered. She did not understand why Jessica was saying this.

"Uh-oh. Excuse us," Jessica said quickly. "I think Elizabeth and I had better check the kitchen again. I smell something funny."

Jessica grabbed Elizabeth by the sleeve and pulled her through the kitchen door.

"I smell something funny too," Elizabeth said angrily. "Why are you telling lies about Steven?"

"Shhhh," Jessica hissed. She peeped around the door to make sure nobody could overhear. "Janet is such a know-it-all! She always has to be right! Maybe I can make a bet with her and prove her wrong for once!"

"What do you mean?" Elizabeth whispered.

"I mean, I think I see a way we might both get to go to see *Staying Up with Bob*. Just play along with me." Jessica giggled loudly, raising her voice so it could be heard in the living room. "Oh, you're right, Elizabeth. I forgot about the girl at the beach last summer."

Elizabeth followed Jessica into the living room.

"Steven can't keep any girl on his mind for long," Jessica continued. "He'll forget all about Jill Hale by next week."

"You've got to be kidding me, Jessica! He's a goner for sure," Janet said haughtily.

"Wanna bet?" Jessica asked quickly.

Janet paused for a minute. "Sure," she said. "What's the bet?"

"You give me one week to prove that Steven is over Jill Hale. If I do, you give both tickets to *Staying Up with Bob* to me and Elizabeth."

Lila gasped. "Don't do it, Janet!"

"No, Janet! If you lose, that means none of us gets to go," Ellen Riteman added.

"I won't lose," Janet said, giving Jessica a smug look. "It's just too bad that Jessica and Elizabeth are only in the sixth grade. They don't understand men like I do. If they did, they wouldn't make such a stupid bet."

"Then we're on?" Jessica asked.

"Let me get this straight," Janet said. "You get one week to prove that Steven is over Jill Hale?" She looked at her watch. "That means by four o'clock next Tuesday?"

"Right."

"And if you do, I give you both *Staying Up with Bob* tickets?"

"That's right," Jessica said.

"If you lose," Janet asked, "what do I get?"

Elizabeth had been wondering that too. What

could Jessica offer that came anywhere close to *Staying Up with Bob* tickets?

Without hesitating, Jessica leaned over and picked up the camera from the coffee table. "A brand-new camera," she said proudly, carefully avoiding Elizabeth's eyes.

Two

◇

"How dare you bet *my* camera?" Elizabeth screamed as soon as Jessica had said goodbye to the last Unicorn.

"It was the first thing I thought of," Jessica said calmly. "And don't worry—we're going to win this bet."

"You could have bet your cassette deck," Elizabeth pointed out. "It's almost brand new."

Jessica bit her lip pensively. "But if I lost it, I wouldn't have any way to play my Johnny Buck tapes."

Elizabeth rolled her eyes and sighed. "And if we lose my camera, I won't have any way to take pictures. Besides, if you think we're going to win this you should have bet something of yours!"

"And we *are* going to win, Elizabeth. Trust me—" Jessica broke off as Steven wandered into the living room.

He stopped in the middle of the room and looked around. Then he sighed and scratched his head.

"Looking for something?" Elizabeth asked.

Steven stared at Elizabeth blankly. "What?"

"Are you looking for something?"

Steven shook his head as if he were waking from a nap. "Uh—yeah . . . I came in here to get something . . . but now I can't remember what it was." He looked at Jessica. "Are your friends gone?"

"Yes," Jessica replied.

"Good," Steven said. He scratched his head again and sighed. Finally he picked up a section of the newspaper and trudged toward the stairs. The twins sat quietly, listening to Steven's heavy footsteps. Just as he reached the stairs, the phone rang.

Elizabeth got up to answer it, but before she was even out of her seat, she heard Steven stomp up the stairs to reach the extension at the top.

"Hello," the twins heard him say in his froggy voice.

Elizabeth had to put a pillow over her face to

muffle her laughter. She kept the pillow pressed to her face as she listened to Steven take a message for Mr. Wakefield.

When she heard the door to his room close with a distant thud, she lifted her face out of the pillow and laughed helplessly. "Poor Steven," she said through her giggles.

Jessica's face was red from subduing her laughter too. "Our own brother is going crazy, and all we can do is laugh," she said seriously. "I didn't just get us into this bet so we could get Janet's tickets. I got us into it to help Steven too. Face it, Elizabeth, he's a basket case. Do you want to see him walking around like a zombie for the rest of his life?"

"He does need help," Elizabeth agreed, pulling herself together.

"He sure does. I can't believe you're worrying about your silly camera when Steven's happiness is at stake!"

Elizabeth looked at her sister for a second, outraged. Then she burst into laughter again. She was always amazed at how Jessica could make the most ridiculous things seem reasonable.

Jessica smiled. "What's important is that we got Janet to take the bet."

"What's important is that we have to *win* the

bet," Elizabeth corrected. "Do you even have a plan?"

"Well, no, not yet," Jessica admitted sheepishly. "But if we put our heads together, we'll come up with something. We always have before. Where's the old twins spirit?"

Elizabeth sat down on the sofa. "This is crazy. We told Janet that we would prove Steven is over Jill Hale by four o'clock next Tuesday. How can we *prove* something like that?"

"Simple," Jessica replied, holding up Elizabeth's camera. "We'll provide photographic evidence—a picture of Steven with somebody else."

"But who?" Elizabeth asked. "Steven hardly even talks to any other girls."

"He talks to Cathy Connors," Jessica said.

"But Cathy's just his friend. And it's too bad, too, because Cathy would be perfect for Steven. She's pretty, they're in the same grade, she's in the band—"

"And they're both interested in sports," Jessica added. "Cathy's the goalie on the girls' hockey team."

Elizabeth smiled. "She laughs at Steven's jokes—even the really awful ones. Now that's a *real* friend." Then she frowned. "But I don't think Steven ever thinks of her as a girlfriend."

Jessica raised her eyebrows. "Neither did Troy," she said.

"Who's Troy?" asked Elizabeth.

"*Troy*. You know. From *Days of Turmoil*," Jessica said. *Days of Turmoil* was Jessica's favorite soap opera. "Pamela was in love with Troy for years, but he never thought of her as anything but a friend," Jessica explained. "Pamela tried everything to get Troy to fall in love with her, but nothing worked. She finally gave up and started dating Troy's best friend, Don. It was only when she married Don that Troy realized that he had been in love with Pamela all along."

Elizabeth shook her head. "But Steven's best friend is Joe Howell, and he's already dating Jill Hale. It would be hard enough to get Steven interested in Cathy. I don't see how we're going to get *Joe* interested in Cathy too."

"Elizabeth!" Jessica yelled. "You're missing the point. We have to make Steven *jealous*. If someone else—say, a secret admirer—started paying attention to Cathy, then Steven might realize what a great girl she is."

"But Cathy doesn't have a secret admirer," Elizabeth pointed out.

"That's where we come in," Jessica said confidently.

Steven lay on his bed staring at the ceiling. He was supposed to be working on an essay for English class, but all he could think about was Jill Hale.

He groaned out loud and buried his head in a pillow. Every time he got near her, he made a complete fool of himself. Just thinking about their date made him cringe with embarrassment.

The disaster date began when he bought her earrings that she already had. Then he took her to a stuffy restaurant where the waiter had treated him like a little kid. The worst part was when he'd had to ask Jill for some money—he hadn't had enough to pay the check! He had done everything completely wrong, and now Jill was going out with Joe Howell.

Still, Jill didn't act like she totally hated him. Maybe if he could get a grip on himself when he was around her, she'd realize he wasn't a complete geek.

Steven got off his bed and looked at himself in the mirror. He didn't think he was bad looking—tall, brown eyes, brown hair. He smiled his biggest smile into the mirror. "Hi, Jill," he said, working hard to keep his voice relaxed and friendly. "How's it going?"

Good, he thought, *but not perfect*, and he decided to keep practicing in front of the mirror until he got it right.

Three

◇

Steven felt pretty happy as he moved through the lunch line in the cafeteria on Wednesday. He'd seen Jill twice that morning in the halls, and both times he had managed to speak to her without tripping over his shoelaces or spitting when he talked. He whistled happily as he took his tray and sat down next to Joe. "Hi, buddy. What's doing?"

Joe looked up at Steven. "My head hurts, and my stomach feels queasy."

"Do you think you're coming down with something?" Steven asked sympathetically.

"Yes," Joe said, looking very sad. "I think I'm getting an F on my geometry quiz this afternoon."

Steven laughed so hard, he choked on his

sandwich. "There's a geometry flu going around," he managed to say.

Joe laughed and took a bite of his lasagna. "Jill came over last night so we could study together. But then we started talking and stuff. I guess we didn't spend enough time going over the geometry problems."

Steven nodded. He could understand how it might be hard to keep your mind on geometry when Jill was around. Just *thinking* about her was enough to blow Steven's concentration.

"How's it going with you?" Joe asked.

"Pretty good," Steven responded. "The grades are hanging in there. And the trombone is definitely getting better. It was the slide that was giving me trouble. I was holding it all wrong. See, I was . . ."

Steven put the hand that was holding his sandwich close to his mouth to demonstrate his grip on the horn. He stretched his other hand out and wobbled his arm to indicate his grip on the slide. "I wasn't holding it steady enough."

Just then, Jill Hale appeared behind Joe. "You guys mind if I sit down?" she asked.

Steven's mouth went dry, and he felt his face flush with embarrassment. Just as he was holding a sandwich under his chin and waving his other arm around like a lunatic, Jill had to show up!

Joe turned around and smiled at her. "Have a seat. Steven was just showing me how you're supposed to hold the trombone."

Jill smiled at Steven. "Great. Let me see."

Steven felt silly, but what could he do? "Well, you have to keep a steady grip on the slide," he said. "Then you have to move it like this." Steven thrust his arm forward, and as he did, he knocked the milk carton off of Joe's lunch tray.

Steven watched in horror as the milk carton flew up, turned over, and landed on Jill. Milk spilled all over the front of her shirt and into her lap.

"Oh, *no!*" Jill shrieked, jumping up from her seat. Milk ran down her jeans and splattered on the table.

Steven leaned forward with a napkin just as Joe leaned forward to move his books out of the spreading puddle. There was a loud crack as their heads smacked together.

"Ouch!" they shouted together.

Steven recovered first. He held out some napkins to Jill. "I'm so sorry," he stammered. "I didn't see . . . I mean . . . I should have been . . ."

Jill glared at him for a minute. Then she snatched the napkins out of his hand and ran toward the water fountain.

Steven watched her as she wetted the napkins and wiped the mess off the front of her clothes.

Joe giggled as he held his head with one hand and mopped up the table with the other. "Relax, Steven. It was an accident."

"Accident or not, Jill's clothes are probably ruined," Steven said. For an awful moment he felt as if he might even cry.

"No, they're not," Joe said. "A little milk can't ruin anything."

Steven sighed. "Except my day."

Joe looked embarrassed. "I know it seems like Jill's making a big deal about nothing. But she's really a great girl in a lot of ways."

"I know she's a great girl," Steven said. "And I also know she thinks I'm a jerk."

"No, she doesn't," Joe argued. "Really! She doesn't. OK, she was a little peeved about that time you took her out. But she doesn't hold it against you. She's always telling me how nice she thinks you are."

"Really?" Steven asked. His heart began to lift.

"Really," Joe assured him.

Jill came back to the table and sat down.

"I'm really sorry, Jill," Steven said, smiling at her.

"It's all right," Jill said grudgingly. "Just forget it, OK?"

Steven's face fell. Joe shifted in his seat. Jill looked at him. Joe was obviously uncomfortable.

Finally, Jill seemed to relent. She smiled brightly at Steven. "I'm sorry for being such a grouch. I got all the milk off. I guess I'm just a little nervous about the geometry quiz this afternoon."

"Join the club," Joe said, his face relieved. "Speaking of geometry, I'm going to study hall for a few minutes before class. I want to go over those problems one more time. Do you want to come, Jill?"

Jill opened her lunch bag and took out a carton of yogurt. "I need to eat first. I'm starved. I'll meet you there as soon as I finish my yogurt."

Joe grabbed his books. "See you guys later," he said as he left.

Steven sat there, his heart racing. He was alone with Jill Hale—just as he was always imagining!

But in his imagination, Jill had been hanging on to his every word and smiling. Now that Joe was gone, she just stared off into the distance as if Steven were not even there. Maybe she was embarrassed about having acted so cranky. Or maybe she really did think he was a jerk.

Steven took a deep breath. "I guess I get kind of carried away when I talk about the band," he said. "I just think the trombone is so cool."

Jill paused a minute. "It's OK," she said. "But a trombone sounds like a catfight unless it's played by a professional."

She probably doesn't mean that the way it sounds, Steven thought. Then again, considering that he has just poured a gallon of milk over her, maybe she did. Strike one.

But it ain't over till it's over, he told himself. Time for a switch play. Jump to basketball—that was solid ground. Steven was the star of Sweet Valley High's junior varsity team.

"So," he said, "did you see our last basketball game?"

Jill swallowed a spoonful of yogurt and frowned as if she were trying hard to think. "Basketball," she said. "That's the game with the hoop, right?"

Strike two. Time to let Jill carry the ball. "Do you have any hobbies or extracurriculars?" Steven asked.

Jill's face brightened. Genuine interest made

her face even pinker and prettier than usual. "Rhetoric!" she exclaimed brightly.

Rhetowhat? Steven thought. His mind went completely blank. He couldn't think of one single thing to say.

Jill took another spoonful of her yogurt. "I'm also crazy about motorcycles," she said.

Steven's heart leaped. *Motorcycles!* Steven was wild about motorcycles. He and Jill had something in common after all! Maybe there was hope.

He struggled to keep his face and voice relaxed. "Yeah, I like motorcycles too," he said. "In fact, I've been thinking about buying one."

It wasn't completely a lie. Fantasizing was a lot like thinking, and Steven had been fantasizing for years about owning a motorcycle—despite the fact that his parents had said he would have one over their dead bodies.

"Really!" Jill exclaimed. She looked at Steven, giving him her full attention. She actually looked as if she were impressed. "That's pretty cool. Most people's parents won't even consider letting them have one."

Steven shrugged. "Yeah, well . . ." What could he say? Fortunately, Jill looked at her watch and jumped up.

"I've got to go," she said, picking up her

empty lunch bag and yogurt container. "I need to review the geometry problems before class. See you." She gave Steven a bright smile and hurried off.

Steven stared after her. If Jill was interested in motorcycles, then there was only one thing to do—get a motorcycle.

Steven closed his eyes. In his mind he saw himself racing up to the front of Sweet Valley High on a motorcycle, Jill riding behind him, her arms wrapped around his waist, her blond hair blowing in the wind.

"Wake up, Wakefield," he heard a voice say. Steven jumped. He opened his eyes and saw Cathy Connors grinning at him.

"No sleeping in the cafeteria," she said sternly.

Steven laughed. Normally he'd be embarrassed if somebody caught him sitting there with his eyes closed. But Cathy was a good friend. She might tease him—but she never did it in a mean way like some girls. When Cathy teased him, it made him laugh.

"I guess I didn't get enough sleep," he said quickly, hoping she wouldn't ask him any more questions. He liked Cathy a lot, but that didn't mean he was ready to tell her about his feelings for Jill. "What's up?"

"Remember I told you about the European trip for the girls' hockey team?"

He didn't remember, but he nodded anyway.

"I'm determined to go, and I figured out how to raise the money. I got a job at McRobert's in the mall. I've been working there a week."

Cathy unwrapped her sandwich and offered half of it to Steven. Steven shook his head, and as Cathy went on, her voice was bright with enthusiasm. "My parents were really against it at first," she said. "They were worried about my grades. But I finally convinced them that having a job would give me a better sense of responsibility and teach me the value of money—parents *love* that stuff. Anyway, I'm working there after school and on weekends."

Steven nodded again, but he wasn't really listening. Luckily, Cathy didn't seem to notice. She just kept talking. In his imagination, Steven was far away from the Sweet Valley High cafeteria. He was roaring through the country on a bright red motorcycle with Jill Hale.

After school, Jessica and Elizabeth walked to the art supply shop and bought some gold foil for step one of their plan. As they were going into the shop, they heard someone calling them.

Elizabeth looked over in the direction of the voice. Caroline Pearce was waving at them. She was standing in front of the Dairi Burger with her sister, Anita, a freshman at Sweet Valley High, Janet Howell, and Kimberly Haver.

The twins joined the other girls at the curb. "Hi," Jessica said. "What's up?"

Janet nudged Anita. "Tell them what you told me."

"You mean about Steven?" Anita's voice was breathless with excitement. Like Caroline, she loved talking about other people's business. "Well, I just thought you ought to know—since he's your brother and everything—that he's really been acting weird lately."

Jessica frowned.

"Today at lunch, I saw Steven accidentally dump his milk all over Jill Hale. He was so embarrassed, he turned *purple*."

Janet laughed and gave the twins a pointed look. "Your brother is a real charmer. My diagnosis is a bad case of Jill Hale-itis."

"With little chance of recovery," Kimberly added.

As the rest of them giggled, Elizabeth grabbed Jessica by the arm and yanked her toward the art supply store.

"This is getting serious," Elizabeth whispered. "You'd better start saving up to buy me a new camera, Jess."

Jessica tried to look confident. "Not so fast, Elizabeth. Just wait till we get Project Get Rid of Jill under way."

Four

◇

After school, Steven stopped off at the newsstand and looked through the racks for motorcycle magazines. There were at least fifteen different titles.

"Can I help you find something?" asked the man behind the counter.

"I was just looking for a motorcycle magazine," Steven answered. "I didn't realize there were so many to choose from. I guess a lot of people like motorcycles."

The man smiled. "Who doesn't?"

My parents, Steven thought. Then he pushed the thought to the back of his mind. If a motorcycle was the way to Jill's heart, then he had to get one!

"What kind of motorcycle are you interested in?" the man asked. "Maybe I can help you pick out the right magazine. I'm a motorcycle buff myself.''

"I don't really know much about them," Steven admitted. "So I guess I want something that can just give me an overview—maybe some information on the best kind to buy."

"Then I'd recommend this one." The man took a magazine from the rack and handed it to Steven. "It's got a lot of real basic information, and there are some ads for used bikes in the back. If you're a first-time buyer, you'll probably want to get one secondhand."

"That's a great idea," Steven said, digging into his wallet for some money.

The man rang up Steven's purchase and dropped the magazine in a bag. "My name's Pete. If you have any questions, drop by again. I love to talk about motorcycles."

"Thanks. I will," Steven said and hurried out the door.

As soon as he got home, Steven ran upstairs to his room. He flopped on his bed and opened the magazine. The very first article was called, "So You're Thinking About Buying a Motorcycle."

Steven eagerly scanned the article, but as soon as he'd read the first paragraph, he began to feel discouraged. The article said you had to be sixteen years old in most states to get a motorcycle license. That meant he'd have to wait two years before he could actually drive one.

I might have to be sixteen to drive a motorcycle, but I don't have to be sixteen to buy one, he thought. If he bought one now, he could keep it in the garage. That way, Jill could come over and look at it. Maybe they could even sit on the seat and pretend they were roaring through Sweet Valley.

Steven read on. By the time he finished the article, he felt that he had a pretty good idea of what he was interested in. Now all he had to do was check his "bank" and then the classified ads.

Steven went to his closet and began digging through piles of laundry, shoes, and papers. His "bank" was an old athletic sock that he was always careful to hide. Sometimes he hid it so well he couldn't find it himself. The room was usually a mess by the time he finally found it.

Steven felt the heavy sock with satisfaction. He had been saving up, doing extra work around the house for the last two weeks, and the sock felt nice and full. He emptied the sock out on his bed and began counting. There was $30.42—fifteen dollars in bills and the rest in change.

Steven was surprised. He had thought he had more. Then again, that date with Jill had really set him back.

He put the money back into the sock and tossed it onto the pile of dirty clothes. He'd put it all away later.

Then he turned to the classified ads and began looking through the "For Sale" section. His eyes widened. Even used motorcycles were expensive—a lot more expensive than $30.42.

Grabbing a pencil and paper, he did some quick calculating. Even if he saved every single penny of his allowance for a year, he still would not have enough money for a motorcycle.

Visions of sitting on a motorcycle in the garage with Jill disappeared. This was going to take longer than he thought. The only way he could put enough money together was by getting a job.

The more Steven thought about it, the better the idea seemed. Mr. and Mrs. Wakefield were definitely not going to like the idea of a motorcycle. But if Steven bought one with his own money, how could they tell him he couldn't have it?

But what if his parents didn't want him to get a job? They would be bound to worry about his grades and stuff. Steven frowned. He tried to remember what Cathy had said to her parents. Something about developing a sense of responsibility and learning the value of money—that was it. If it worked on Cathy's parents, why wouldn't it work on Mr. and Mrs. Wakefield?

Steven went to the mirror. He looked at himself, trying to imagine that he was speaking to his parents.

Out loud he said, "Please, Dad. I've got to learn about responsibility *sometime*."

Too whiny, he thought.

"Gosh, Mom. Don't you think it's time I developed a stronger sense of responsibility?"

Too boyish.

"I've given it a lot of thought, and I really think it's time I had a job and learned for myself the value of money."

Better. Much better.

"I hope we're not making a mistake," Elizabeth said as she picked up her purse and jacket.

Jessica sighed impatiently. "You're not going to chicken out now, are you?"

"No," Elizabeth said doubtfully. "But we *are* interfering with Steven's love life. If this backfires, it could create a lot of problems. I just wish I were sure that we're doing the right thing."

"We're doing the right thing," Jessica said confidently.

"For us or for Steven?" Elizabeth asked.

Jessica grinned. "Both. I'll get my purse and meet you downstairs."

As Elizabeth started down the stairs, she heard a voice coming from Steven's room. *I didn't know Steven had company*, she thought as she stopped at the top of the stairs. *I wonder who he's talking to.*

She tiptoed to the door of Steven's room. It was open just a crack, so she peeped in. There was Steven, all alone, standing in front of the mirror. He was making faces and talking very earnestly to his own reflection. Elizabeth struggled to hear what he was saying. She couldn't make out the words, but it sounded as if he were having an argument with himself.

"What are you doing?" Jessica whispered in her ear.

Elizabeth jumped and put a finger to her lips. She tiptoed down the stairs, pulling Jessica behind her.

As soon as they were safely out the front door, Elizabeth turned toward her sister. "Now he's up there talking to himself. He's making really strange faces too."

"Good grief—he really *is* going crazy," Jessica said. "See, Elizabeth? We *are* doing the right thing."

Fifteen minutes later, the twins were inside the Sweet Valley Florist. A pleasant woman greeted them with a smile. "Good afternoon, girls."

"Good afternoon," Elizabeth replied. "We would like to order some flowers to be delivered to this address." She handed the florist a piece of paper. "Can you do that?"

"Of course," the lady said, looking at the address. "What kind of flowers did you want to send?"

Jessica spoke up. "Roses. A dozen red roses."

"How lovely," the lady said. She opened the door of a refrigerated case. The smell of roses filled the air. "We just got these in."

Jessica gasped. "They're beautiful!"

"We have some things we want to send with them. Is that all right?" Elizabeth asked.

The lady took out a long white box and lined the inside with tissue paper. "What would you like to send?"

Elizabeth reached into her pack and pulled out three gold letters—all *E*s. She had cut them out of cardboard and covered them with the gold foil. "Will these fit in the box?"

The lady laid them carefully in the top of the box. "They fit perfectly."

"There's a note that needs to go with it. Do you have a card?"

"Certainly." The lady smiled. She handed Elizabeth a small white card. Elizabeth took a pen from her purse. She wrote very slowly, speaking aloud as she drew the elaborate letters.

> Letter by letter . . .
> You'll know better . . .
> Who admires you.

"Do I detect a romance?" the florist asked.

Jessica smiled brightly. "Yes. We're sending these for this very handsome and romantic man. He's in love with a beautiful woman, but he's too shy to tell her. This is his way of courting her."

The florist looked fascinated, so Jessica went on. "He's going to send her a series of gifts. And with every gift, he'll send her a few more letters of his name. By the time she gets all the letters and learns his identity, he's hoping she'll be as madly in love with him as he is with her."

Elizabeth smiled to herself. She and Jessica had worked hard on their plan, and they were both very proud of it.

The florist laughed. "Just when I was beginning to think romance was dead. I'm glad to see I was wrong. That will be twenty-five dollars and sixty-five cents."

Elizabeth's heart sank. She looked at Jessica's face. It mirrored her own disappointment. They didn't have nearly enough money. "Uh," she said, "I'm afraid—" She broke off as Jessica jumped in.

"I'm afraid that's more than he can afford," she said apologetically. "He's a poet, as you could probably tell from the poem. So he doesn't have much money. Do you have anything less expensive?"

The lady put the roses back into the case. "The tulips are on sale for a dollar and a quarter a piece."

Elizabeth did some quick figuring in her head. She and Jessica had pooled their money to finance this project. Together, they had about seventeen dollars. If they spent all their money on the first gift, they wouldn't be able to send gifts to go with the rest of the letters. "We'll take ten," she said.

There would not be much money left over, but Elizabeth wanted the first gift to be impressive.

Elizabeth watched as the florist selected the blooms and laid them in the box—"nine . . . ten . . . eleven, twelve."

Elizabeth spoke up quickly. "Oh, just ten, please. That's all we—I mean, *he*—can afford."

The florist smiled as she closed the box. "I know. But twelve is a much more romantic number than ten, don't you think? The extra two are on the house—for the sake of romance."

"Oh, thank you!" the girls said together.

Elizabeth paid, and Jessica thanked her again.

"My pleasure," the florist said, her eyes twinkling. "I hope this young poet succeeds in winning his lady."

"He will," Jessica assured her as they left the shop.

Once they were outside, Elizabeth broke into a fit of giggles. "You should be a writer, Jessica. Picturing Steven as a romantic poet takes a lot of imagination. Maybe you could write for *Days of Turmoil*."

"*Days of Poverty* would be more like it," Jessica said. "Romance sure is expensive. We're almost broke, and we've got twelve letters to go."

Five

◇

"Who would have thought the word *job* would start World War III in the Wakefield house," Steven said.

It was Thursday, and Steven and Cathy were sitting in the cafeteria. "I knew my folks would be against it at first," he said. "But I didn't realize they'd have conniptions."

"What did they say?" Cathy asked.

"Mainly that they were worried about my grades, the band, and basketball."

"Can you really do all those things and work too?"

"Sure," Steven said cheerfully. "Band practice is only one afternoon a week, and basketball season is almost over. I've got lots of free time. Why shouldn't I use the extra time for a part-time job?"

"So your parents said it was OK?" Cathy asked.

"Eventually," Steven answered. "I had to do a lot of fast talking. But what really clinched it was using your lines."

Cathy looked puzzled. "My lines?"

Steven laughed. "You know, that stuff about learning the value of money and developing a sense of responsibility. I even added a few touches of my own. I said that lots of great men worked while they were growing up—and hard work and determination had molded them into world leaders and captains of industry."

Cathy laughed so hard, she choked on her milk. "How corny can you get!"

Steven looked embarrassed. "It might be corny, but it worked."

"Why are you in such a hurry?" Cathy asked. "Why not wait until summer?"

"You sound like my folks!" Steven objected.

"Well, why *not* wait until summer?"

Steven took a sip of his milk. "Because if I wait until summer, there's so much competition, it's impossible to find a job."

Cathy nodded. Steven was glad that she seemed satisfied with his answer. He definitely did not want to tell her about the motorcycle and

Jill. "So anyway, they finally said I could have a job—but only if I keep up my grades *and* only if I take the job seriously. That means I can't quit just because I get bored."

Cathy nodded again. "Do you want me to see if they need anyone else at McRobert's?" she asked.

"Forget it! I wouldn't be caught dead working in one of those places. Flipping burgers is definitely not my thing."

Cathy looked down at her notebook and absently flipped the pages. She didn't say anything. There was a long silence.

Steven felt like kicking himself. "I'm sorry, Cathy. I didn't mean that the way it sounded."

Cathy looked up. "What?"

"I didn't mean that the way it sounded."

Cathy frowned. "Mean what the way it sounded?"

"What I said about McRobert's."

"I'm sorry." Cathy laughed. "I guess I was thinking about something else. What did you say about McRobert's?"

Steven sighed impatiently. "I was just saying that I'd rather have a . . . more interesting job. I think I'd be a good lifeguard. What do you think?"

Cathy didn't answer.

"Cathy?" he prompted.

Cathy still didn't answer.

"Cathy!" he shouted.

Cathy jumped. "What?"

"Are you mad at me or something?" Steven asked.

Cathy looked guilty. "No, of course not. I guess I wasn't paying attention. I'm sorry. I was just thinking about—" Cathy broke off as Anita Pearce sat down next to her.

"So who's sending you flowers?" Anita demanded.

"How did you know about that?"

"I saw the florist van outside your house yesterday afternoon," Anita said with a smirk. "I asked the delivery man who was getting the flowers. He said they were for 'Ms. Cathy Connors.'"

Steven rolled his eyes. He thought Anita Pearce was the nosiest person in the world. He hoped Cathy would really tell her off.

Much to his surprise, Cathy just giggled. "You should be a detective someday," she said.

Steven could not believe it. *Why doesn't Cathy tell her to mind her own business?*

"Tell me everything!" Anita said. "I'm dying of curiosity."

Steven looked at Cathy again. She didn't look angry at all. She looked pleased and kind of embarrassed.

"It's a secret admirer," Cathy said. "He sent me this note—and these letters." Cathy pulled the three *E*s from her notebook and the note Elizabeth had written. She put it on the table for Steven and Anita to read.

"Oh, how romantic!" Anita exclaimed.

"What a jerk!" Steven thought Cathy had lost her mind. "For all you know, this guy could be an ax murderer."

Anita and Cathy giggled.

Steven frowned. "I'm serious. You'd better be careful, Cathy."

Anita and Cathy broke into peals of laughter.

Steven shook his head in bewilderment. Cathy had always seemed so sensible. Now she was getting to be like all the other girls—silly.

"It sounds to me like you're jealous, Steven Wakefield," Anita teased.

Steven glared at Anita, then got up and left the table in disgust. *Let them giggle over some stupid anonymous note*, he thought. He had better things to do—he had to find a job!

*   *   *

As soon as school was over, Steven jumped onto his bike and rode to the Sweet Valley public swimming pool. The pool was a hangout for a lot of kids at Sweet Valley High. Steven thought working there as a lifeguard would definitely be fun.

He walked across the grounds toward the manager's office. He paused outside the door and took a deep breath, then knocked.

"Come in," a voice said.

Steven opened the door and stepped inside. He recognized the man behind the desk as Mr. Clarkson, the manager of the pool for as long as he could remember.

Mr. Clarkson smiled. "I know you," he said.

"Hi, Mr. Clarkson. I'm Steven Wakefield."

The man seemed to be thinking hard. "Aren't you the fellow with the twin sisters?"

Steven laughed. "That's right."

The manager smiled again. "They must make life interesting for you."

Steven laughed.

"What can I do for you, Steven?" he asked.

"I'm looking for a job," Steven said. "I was wondering if you needed a lifeguard."

"We sure do," Mr. Clarkson replied.

Steven's heart leaped.

"Do you have a lifesaving certificate?" Mr. Clarkson asked.

"No," Steven answered. "But—"

Mr. Clarkson shook his head. "I can't hire you without a lifesaving certificate."

"I'm a really good swimmer," Steven argued. "I've been swimming all my life. I've even pulled my sisters out of the pool once or twice."

The manager looked at Steven sympathetically. "I'm sure you're a very competent young man," he said. "But by law, I can't hire you without a lifesaving certificate." Mr. Clarkson thought for a moment. "You know, we'll be giving classes in life saving this summer. If you take the class and pass it, you'll qualify for the certificate. Then I'd be happy to talk to you about a job."

"But that's too late," Steven said.

"Too late?"

Steven stared at his feet. "I just need a job sooner," he mumbled.

The manager sensed Steven's disappointment. "I do need somebody a couple afternoons a week in the snack shop," he offered. "Would you be interested in that?"

"You mean making burgers and stuff?"

Steven asked. That was exactly what he had been determined *not* to do.

Mr. Clarkson nodded.

"Thanks, but I think I'll look around a little more. I was really hoping for something a little . . . uh . . . more responsible."

Mr. Clarkson chuckled. "I understand. There's not much glamour in the burger business, is there? You know, I believe that Valley Music is hiring. Why don't you try them?"

Steven brightened. "Thanks a lot, Mr. Clarkson," he said. "I will."

Twenty minutes later, Steven parked his bike in front of Valley Music. He was sweating as he locked his bicycle to the rack. It was going to be hard to make a good impression after bicycling six miles in the heat.

He pulled a towel out of his gym bag and quickly wiped his face. Then he ran a comb through his hair and checked to make sure his shirt was tucked in.

He noticed with satisfaction that a "Help Wanted" sign was hanging in the window. Steven went inside and asked for the manager. A few minutes later, he was introducing himself to a Mr. Gomez.

"I need someone on weekends and a couple of afternoons a week. Would that fit your schedule?" Mr. Gomez asked.

"That would be perfect," Steven said.

"And I need somebody who knows a lot about music."

No problem, Steven thought. Jessica was always entering some kind of "Name That Tune" contest, and she was always playing records over and over until she—and every member of the Wakefield family—knew them by heart.

"I know a lot about music," Steven assured him. "We have music playing in our house all the time. I also play the trombone in the school band."

Mr. Gomez looked pleased. "That's good. Our salespeople have to be knowledgeable. Quite often, customers have questions about different recordings, and they rely on our advice."

Steven nodded. That made a lot of sense. In his mind, he pictured Jill Hale coming into the store to buy a record. Steven would step forward and make a recommendation. Jill would smile up at him gratefully.

Suddenly, Steven realized that Mr. Gomez was asking him a question. "I'm sorry," Steven said. "What did you say?"

Mr. Gomez was pointing to a bin of records. "I was asking you how long you thought it would take you to pull out the baroque recordings and set up a separate section?"

Pull out the what recordings? Steven thought.

Mr. Gomez took in Steven's blank stare. "You *do* know classical music, don't you?"

"Uh, our band doesn't play much classical music," Steven admitted.

Mr. Gomez looked disappointed. Then he brightened. "Well, if you play the trombone, you must know a lot about jazz."

Steven racked his brains, but he couldn't think of a single jazz musician he knew anything about.

"New age?" asked Mr. Gomez hopefully. "Big band? Opera?"

All Steven could do was shake his head.

"Well what kind of music *do* you know about?"

"I know every tune in the top forty," Steven announced proudly.

Mr. Gomez laughed. "I'm sorry, Steven. But top forty is just one small area of music. Being able to identify the songs in the top forty doesn't make you knowledgeable about music."

Steven blushed. He felt like an idiot.

"I'm sorry to laugh," Mr. Gomez said as he walked Steven to the door. "And I can see you're serious about wanting to work. Why don't you try one of the burger places in the mall?"

Steven thanked Mr. Gomez, but inside he was seething. Why was everyone in such a hurry to put him in the burger business? Couldn't they see that he had real ambition?

Steven stepped back out into the heat, feeling tired and angry. As he was unlocking his bicycle, Mr. Gomez stuck his head out the door. "Steven," he called, "I just thought of something else. Valley Computers is looking for part-time help. Why don't you try them? They're right next to the Sweet Valley pool."

Steven's spirits lifted. It meant another long bike trip, but if he could get a job, it would be worth it.

"Know anything about computers?" the store manager of Valley Computers asked, looking up from his computer terminal.

"Uh, not really," Steven answered. "But I could learn."

"Not on my time," the manager said curtly, turning back to the terminal.

Steven couldn't believe how rude this guy was. He wished he could tell him off, but he was getting desperate. He really needed a job. "Please give me a chance," he persisted.

The man looked up from his terminal again and sighed. "Look, kid, I've already got a stock boy. What I need is someone who can handle sales and programming. If you don't know anything about computers, you can't help me. If I were you, I'd try the mall. Those fast-food places hire a lot of unskilled workers."

The manager turned back to his computer. The conversation was over.

Steven gritted his teeth. *Unskilled!* He was a good student and a great athlete. Why couldn't people give him credit for being intelligent and willing to work hard?

Steven's shoulders sagged. He turned and headed toward the door.

"Rough day?" a voice asked him.

Steven looked up and saw one of the clerks looking at him sympathetically. "Yeah," Steven said, giving him a rueful smile. "I've been looking for a job, and I can't find one. Your manager seems to think I'm an *unskilled worker.*"

The clerk smiled. "He didn't mean to insult you," he said. "But you have to look at it from his perspective. You haven't finished your education. So unless you have some kind of specific expertise to offer, you *are* unskilled in terms of work experience. If I were you, I'd try one of the burger places," he offered helpfully.

Steven struggled hard to keep his voice polite. The man was just trying to be helpful. "Thanks," Steven said as he stepped back out into the heat. "Maybe I will."

But as he unlocked his bike, he thought he'd rather die.

As he pedaled home, the sun beat down on his head and sweat poured down his back. He'd never been so hot and tired in his whole life. He felt like he must have pedaled a hundred miles today.

If only he had a motorcycle—a hundred miles would be a snap if you didn't have to pedal. A motorcycle would just eat up the pavement.

Steven's legs were exhausted. The muscles in his thighs felt like jelly as he pedaled up another hill. Home seemed like a million miles away.

By the time Steven coasted into the Wakefield driveway, his mind was made up. Never again would he go through another day like today. He *had* to get a motorcycle. If he had to flip burgers to get one—then, like it or not, he was going to flip burgers.

Steven trudged into the house and gulped down three glasses of water. Then he went to the telephone and dialed Cathy's number. If Cathy could get him a job at McRobert's, he'd take it.

Six

◇

Elizabeth bent her head backward. Then, very carefully, she placed a Ping-Pong ball on the tip of her nose. Slowly, she removed her hand. Miraculously, the ball stayed put—delicately balanced on the end of her nose. Elizabeth's heart soared.

After a hundred and nineteen unsuccessful attempts, she had finally managed to balance the Ping-Pong ball on her nose. Now for the water.

She reached for the glass of water that she had placed on the desk. She lifted it toward her mouth, being very careful not to move her head and disturb the ball. She lifted the glass higher . . . higher . . . higher . . . and—

"What in the world are you doing?" Jessica asked.

Elizabeth jumped at the sound of Jessica's voice. The Ping-Pong ball slid off her nose, and water from the glass sloshed into her eye.

Elizabeth glared at Jessica. "Don't you ever knock?"

"The door was open," Jessica said defensively. She bent over and picked up the Ping-Pong ball. She looked at Elizabeth curiously. "What's with the Ping-Pong ball?"

Elizabeth wiped the water from her face and grinned. "I'm trying to drink a glass of water while balancing a Ping-Pong ball on my nose."

Jessica blinked, momentarily wondering if her intelligent, practical, sensible twin had lost her mind. Then she began to laugh. "I know what you're doing. You're trying to come up with a stupid stunt, aren't you?"

"Stupid Stunts" was one of the most popular segments on *Staying Up with Bob*. During the show, Bob, the host, would invite audience members to get up on stage and do silly tricks. Elizabeth was secretly dying to be chosen.

Elizabeth sighed. "Yes. But so far, I can't seem to come up with one."

"You're just not the type," Jessica said. "You're way too sensible. Stupid stunts are my department. If I get on the show, I'm going to tie a ribbon with my toes."

Jessica could, in fact, tie a ribbon with her toes—much to the amazement of her friends and family. She had discovered this talent last Christmas while she and Elizabeth were wrapping gifts.

Elizabeth groaned. "You're so lucky, Jessica. I wish I could come up with a goofy and useless talent like that."

"Unfortunately, *all* my talents are useless and goofy. At least your talents are the kind that people respect."

Elizabeth laughed.

"Forget about stupid stunts for now," Jessica said, flopping down on Elizabeth's bed. "We've got to send another present to Cathy and three more letters."

"How much money have we got left?" Elizabeth asked.

Jessica pulled a coin purse from her pocket and emptied the money out onto the bed. It didn't take long to count. "Exactly three dollars and forty-seven cents. We can't get anything decent for that amount of money."

Elizabeth flopped on the bed next to Jessica. "What about sending Cathy the gold letters without a present?"

Jessica shook her head. "No. We don't want the secret admirer to look cheap."

Elizabeth nodded. Jessica was right—a present was essential. But what could they send?

Elizabeth sat up quickly. "I know! Cathy loves chocolate. We can get her a bag of chocolate candies."

Jessica clapped her hands. "That's brilliant. We've sent flowers, and now we'll send candy. It's totally romantic."

"We'll go by her house and sneak them into her mailbox tonight," Elizabeth said.

Jessica scooped the money back into the coin purse. "What are we waiting for!"

All through his classes on Friday, Steven could hardly wait for school to be over. Cathy had told him over the phone to drop by McRobert's at three-thirty if she didn't see him during lunch. He had looked for her in the cafeteria, but she wasn't there. Steven hoped she knew how much he was counting on her.

When the last bell rang, Steven raced out the door of Sweet Valley High. At three-thirty on the dot, he walked into McRobert's and spotted Cathy behind the counter.

Cathy handed a tray of food to a customer. When she looked up and saw Steven, her eyes sparkled. "Do you know anybody named Ed?"

Steven frowned. "I don't think so. Why?"

Cathy pulled a gold *E*, *D*, and *L* from a shelf under the counter. "These were in the mailbox this morning along with a bag of chocolate candies. My secret admirer strikes again. I think the first name could be Ed, but I don't know anybody named Ed. It *could* be letters in the last name. Edelman, maybe." Cathy stared at the letters, moving them around on the counter. "This person has a lot of *E*s in his name."

Steven felt really annoyed. Did Cathy think he had come by to talk about her love life?

Cathy looked up at his face. "What's the matter, Steven?"

"My job?" he reminded her with a frown. "It's kind of important to me."

"Oh," Cathy said. A flicker of disappointment flashed across her face. Steven's heart sank. He thought that she must have bad news.

"I talked to the manager," she said. "He does need someone."

"Yippeee!" Steven shouted. It was just like Cathy to fool him. "You're a pal, Connors."

"The manager's name is Rick. He just ran over to the office supply store for a minute, but he'll be right back. He said if you can train this afternoon, you can start tomorrow."

"You bet I'll train this afternoon!"

"Great," Cathy said. "Here's Rick now."

Steven turned around and saw a sullen-looking young man walking toward them. He looked about nineteen and had bad skin, buck teeth, and a really nerdy tie.

"Hi, Rick," Cathy said. "This is Steven Wake-field. He's the friend I was telling you about."

"Hi," Steven said. "It's nice to meet you."

Steven extended his hand to shake, but Rick ignored it. He looked Steven up and down.

"I think I've got a uniform that will fit you," he said. "It's in the stockroom. Go in there and put it on. I'll meet you back out here in ten minutes." Rick turned and marched into the office at the back.

"What a creep!" Steven exclaimed.

Cathy rolled her eyes. "Tell me about it! He's a business major at Sweet Valley Junior College. He thinks that makes him a real tycoon." She pointed toward the stockroom. "He can be a real grouch if you keep him waiting. You'd better go ahead and change."

Steven went into the stockroom. He didn't like Rick, but he was determined not to let that spoil his happiness. Steven looked around and spotted the uniform hanging on a hook.

Steven quickly stripped off his clothes and began to put the uniform on. He grimaced as he buttoned up the orange and brown polyester shirt. It was hideous. It looked like a linoleum floor after a food fight.

The matching pants were even worse. They felt like they were made out of rubber. Steven looked down and saw that they were at least an inch and a half too short.

An orange hat and a bandanna were pinned to the back pocket. Steven knotted the bandanna around his neck and stuck the hat on his head. Then he turned around to leave.

As he did, he noticed that there was a full-length mirror on the back of the door.

He saw himself and gasped. He looked like a clown! He looked worse than a clown—he looked like a serious nerd! Steven debated with himself for exactly two seconds, then reached a decision.

He began to unbutton the shirt. He'd just tell

Cathy he had changed his mind about the job. Hopefully, she wouldn't be too mad at him. There was no way he was going to be seen in this getup. Not for a motorcycle. Not for Jill. Not for anybody.

There was a knock at the door. "Steven!" Cathy called. "Are you changed? If you are, come out."

Steven opened the door a crack. "If you think I'm coming out in this outfit, you're crazy," he said.

"Don't be ridiculous," Cathy said. "It's not the greatest uniform in the world, but it's not the worst either. You should see what they have to wear at Wurst World—Alpine hats and clogs."

"I don't care," Steven said stubbornly. "I'd rather die than wear this. What if somebody I know sees me?"

Cathy laughed. "So what? When you see me in the uniform, do you think I look awful?"

Cathy had a point. He had never thought about her uniform one way or the other. He began to feel a little better.

"Come on out," Cathy coaxed. "Everybody knows you're a cool guy no matter what you're wearing."

Steven laughed. Cathy was really a great

friend. No matter how down he felt, she could always make him feel better. So what if the uniform was gross? He had a job. That meant he was on his way to owning a motorcycle. How could he have even considered backing out over something as silly as a uniform?

Steven stepped out of the stockroom. He still felt a little self-conscious, but he felt better when he looked at Cathy. She looked fine in her uniform. In fact, she looked kind of cute.

Suddenly, he felt really happy.

"Come here, kid!" Rick shouted. "I'll show you how the deep fryer works. And be careful. I don't want to send you home to your mommy with any burns."

Steven and Cathy looked at each other. They didn't even have to speak. Each knew what the other was thinking—Rick was a jerk.

Cathy winked at Steven. Steven winked back. *Rick or no Rick, it's going to be fun working with Cathy*, Steven thought happily.

Seven

When Jessica woke up on Saturday morning, she could smell bacon frying downstairs. Jessica often slept through breakfast on Saturdays, but last night Elizabeth had insisted that they both get up and go down to breakfast the next morning. That would give them a chance to question Steven a little before he went to work. Steven's new job—working with Cathy—was a great stroke of luck for them. Did this mean the plan was working?

Jessica wasn't sure. Steven hadn't said anything about Cathy's secret admirer. He would have to know about it, though, wouldn't he? He and Cathy were together all the time. But he hadn't shown any signs of being jealous—yet. And he was still hurling himself at the phone every time it rang, answering it in his deep froggy voice.

Jessica yawned. She would give anything to go back to sleep. She looked at the clock. It was strange that Elizabeth hadn't come in to wake her yet. Maybe she was still asleep.

When she peeped through the bathroom door, she saw that Elizabeth was up. She was rummaging through the pockets of a jacket, and there were several more jackets piled on the bed.

"What are you doing?" Jessica asked.

"I'm trying to see if I have any money I've forgotten about. Our 'Get Rid of Jill' fund is down to zilch. That bag of candy left us with only about four cents."

"I don't know," Jessica said. "If Steven's not jealous by now, it's probably not worth spending any more money. Besides, I'm sleepy. Let's go back to bed."

Elizabeth stamped her foot. "Jessica Wakefield, this whole thing was your idea! Don't you dare try to back out now!"

"But if we don't have any money . . ." Jessica began weakly.

"Then we'll just have to think of something else," Elizabeth finished. "I'm not handing my camera over to Janet Howell just because you're too sleepy to put your mind to work. Come on— let's go downstairs and interrogate Steven. And be subtle," she warned.

The twins put on their robes and went downstairs. Mrs. Wakefield and Steven were already at the breakfast table. Mr. Wakefield was standing at the stove frying bacon in one pan and scrambling eggs in another.

"Jessica!" Mrs. Wakefield exclaimed. "This is a surprise. To what do we owe the honor of your presence this Saturday morning?"

Jessica grinned. "I smelled the bacon."

A few minutes later, Mr. Wakefield sat down, placing a platter of bacon and eggs in the center of the table. "Well, help yourself to the McWakefield's breakfast special."

Everyone laughed. Steven piled his plate with bacon and eggs, then enthusiastically dug in.

"So how's the job, Steven?" Elizabeth asked.

"Fine," Steven answered through a mouthful of eggs.

Elizabeth nibbled at a piece of bacon. "How do you like working with Cathy?"

Steven gave her a big smile. "It's great! The manager is a real jerk, but with Cathy around, it's fun anyway. We call him Revolting Rick." He frowned. "Too bad she's not going to be there until afternoon," he added. "I'm working all day today, but she's just working a half shift. It's going to be gruesome until she gets there."

Jessica looked at Elizabeth and lifted her brows.

"We ran into Caroline and Anita Pearce yesterday. Anita said that some secret admirer is sending Cathy presents and stuff," Jessica said, her face carefully bland. "Have you seen any sign of the mystery man?"

Steven's face darkened. "Anita Pearce is such a big mouth. She should mind her own business." He ate for a few more minutes in silence, then pushed his plate away. "May I be excused? I've got to get ready for work."

"Aren't you going to finish your breakfast?" Mrs. Wakefield asked.

"Nah. I'm full," he answered, getting up from the table.

Jessica kicked Elizabeth lightly under the table. Their plan was working. No doubt about it—Steven was jealous! They couldn't quit now. Somehow, they had to get the money to send Cathy another present.

"Uh, Mom," Jessica began, "do you think I could get an advance on my allowance? Just a few dollars."

Mrs. Wakefield frowned. "I thought that your father and I had made it clear that there were going to be no more handouts. Your aunt Helen gave you each a hundred dollars not long ago. There's no reason you should be asking for more money. You're just going to have to learn to budget more efficiently."

Jessica could have kicked herself. Why hadn't she gotten Elizabeth to ask?

Jessica had blown her money at the mall, buying presents for her friends and herself. Steven had thrown his away on a date. Elizabeth had at least saved most of hers and bought a camera. She hadn't squandered it like Jessica and Steven. If Elizabeth had asked for an advance, Mrs. Wakefield might have given it to her.

But now that Mrs. Wakefield had said no to Jessica, she'd feel that she had to say no to Elizabeth too. Jessica looked at Elizabeth and shrugged.

Elizabeth spoke up. "I'm out of money too," she said. "Between the camera and all the film I've bought, I'm broke. Are there any extra chores we could do to earn some money?"

Mrs. Wakefield sighed. "I'm afraid not. You girls are just going to have to tighten your belts and wait for your allowances."

Steven had come back into the kitchen in time to hear the end of the conversation. He was dressed and ready for work. "I've got a chore for you, if you're interested."

"What is it?" Jessica asked.

"My laundry. I've got a ton of it. I just cleaned out my gym locker. I'll pay you a dollar if you'll wash it and fold it up."

"No way!" Jessica exclaimed. "One dollar— to do all that gross laundry!"

"A dollar fifty," Steven said. "That's my final offer. Take it or leave it."

"We'll take it, on one condition," Elizabeth said quickly. "You pay in advance."

Steven reached into his pocket and pulled out six quarters. "Done deal."

Mr. Wakefield cleared his throat. "Far be it from me to act as a barrier to free trade," he said to Steven, "but I don't want you to make a habit of hiring your sisters to do your chores. We agreed to let you work only as long as you fulfilled all your other obligations. Remember?"

"It's just this one time," Steven promised. "Once I get into a regular routine, I'll get everything done. But today's my first full day of work. I didn't expect to start this soon."

"All right then," Mr. Wakefield agreed.

After breakfast the twins raced upstairs to Elizabeth's room. "It's working!" Elizabeth said excitedly. "Steven acted really upset when you mentioned Cathy's secret admirer."

"He sure did. I've never seen him leave food on a plate before. We've got to send Cathy another present and some more letters. And we've got to do it today—before she goes to work. That way, she'll be sure to mention it to Steven this afternoon."

Jessica jingled the six quarters. "What can we get for a lousy dollar fifty?"

"The drugstore sells helium balloons made out of silver plastic," Elizabeth said. "They're a dollar each. Some of them have hearts on them. Why don't we get one of those and tie the letters to the string? Then we can attach it to Cathy's mailbox. She'll see it when she leaves for work."

"That's a great idea!" Jessica said.

"I'll cut out the letters and get them ready," Elizabeth said. "You go throw Steven's laundry in the washer."

Jessica paused, tapping her fingers on Elizabeth's desk. "Uh . . . I think I'd better get dressed if we're going to the—"

"*Jessica!*" Elizabeth said. "You go throw Steven's laundry into the washer."

"OK, OK." Jessica raced into Steven's room and scooped all the clothes up off the floor. She carried them down to the basement and threw them into the washing machine. Then she added a cup of soap powder and turned on the machine.

As soon as the cycle started, the machine began to make a strange thumping sound. Alarmed, Jessica opened the top of the washer and peered inside. Everything looked normal, so what was making that sound?

Jessica reached her arm into the washer and felt around. Her hand closed over a heavy, wet object.

Jessica fished it out and recognized one of Steven's old gym socks. It was stuffed with something heavy and tied in a knot. That something felt a lot like coins. Quickly, Jessica untied the knot.

"Oh, my gosh!" she said as the money spilled out. She sat down and counted it. There were fifteen soggy one-dollar bills—and at least another ten in change. It was more than enough for a gift today, tomorrow, and the next day.

Too bad the money was Steven's.

Or was it?

Jessica turned the machine back on. As it sloshed and hummed, she had an idea. The

Wakefield family had a "finders, keepers" policy when it came to things found in the washing machine.

Once Jessica had left a lipstick in the pocket of her jeans. Her mother had thrown them into the washer with some of her own clothes, and everything had come out covered with greasy pink spots.

That night at dinner, Mrs. Wakefield had announced the new policy. From now on, she had said, anything found in the washer was the property of the finder—jewelry, keys, hair clips, and money.

It had been a joke, really—a way to get them to check their pockets before throwing clothes in the laundry. So far, nobody had found more than a quarter and a few bobby pins. But this was big money. Policy or no policy, Elizabeth would probably insist that Jessica return the money.

On the other hand, it wasn't really any of Elizabeth's business. Jessica had found the money. Technically, it was hers.

Jessica took the laundry out of the washer and put it into the dryer. Even though they would be using the money for Steven's benefit, she knew Elizabeth well enough to know she would refuse to touch it. Jessica would just have to figure out some way to keep Elizabeth from finding out about it.

Maybe she could manage to get to the drugstore by herself and buy a whole bunch of balloons for Cathy? Elizabeth would never even have to know.

Jessica darted upstairs to her room. She stuck the bills into the pocket of her jeans and stashed the change in a drawer.

She noticed that Elizabeth had put a Johnny Buck cassette into Jessica's tape deck. The hit single "The Walls Have Ears" was turned up full blast.

The connecting door that led to the twins' bathroom was open so that the music could be heard from Elizabeth's room.

Jessica went through the bathroom into Elizabeth's room and was startled to find her twin standing in front of the mirror making strange faces. It looked as if she were opening her eyes and lifting her eyebrows in time to the music.

"What are you doing?" Jessica asked.

"As I was cutting out letters, I suddenly had a new idea for a stupid stunt," Elizabeth said. "Does it look like my ears are wiggling?"

Jessica watched Elizabeth carefully. "No," she said. "It looks like your *eyes* are wiggling."

Elizabeth groaned. "I was hoping I could wiggle my ears to 'The Walls Have Ears.' That would be a really good stupid stunt, wouldn't it?"

"It would," Jessica agreed, "*if* you could wiggle your ears. Maybe you should write to Johnny Buck and ask him to change the words to 'The Walls have *Eyes*.'"

"Very funny," Elizabeth said.

"Steven's clothes are in the dryer," Jessica said, trying hard to sound casual. "Why don't you give me the letters? I'll go to the drugstore and get the balloon. You can stay here and fold the clothes when they're dry."

"I have a better idea," Elizabeth countered. "Why don't *I* go to the drugstore and *you* stay here and fold the clothes?"

"I washed them and put them in the dryer," Jessica argued. "The least you can do is take them out and fold them."

"I did the negotiating and cut out the letters," Elizabeth insisted stubbornly. "The least you could do is finish the laundry."

Jessica shifted uncomfortably. There were times when Elizabeth just refused to be manipulated. "Why don't we both go to the drugstore, and we'll fold the laundry when we get home?" Jessica said finally.

Elizabeth grinned at her. "Done deal. Let's move."

Twenty minutes later, the twins were locking their bicycles to the rack outside the Valley Pharmacy.

"Elizabeth! Jessica!" The twins turned as they heard Amy Sutton's voice. Amy was standing outside the drugstore with another girl. Both of them were holding bags from the pharmacy.

"What's Amy doing with Melissa McCormick?" Jessica whispered.

"I think they're doing a school project together," Elizabeth answered. Melissa had taken ballet lessons with the twins, but the twins didn't know her very well. She always seemed shy to them.

"Hi, Melissa. Hi, Amy," Elizabeth said, walking over. "What did you buy?"

Melissa gave the twins a shy smile. "I came to pick up some tape for my brother. He twisted his ankle playing basketball, and he has to keep it wrapped for a couple of weeks."

"Your brother must be Andy McCormick," Elizabeth said. "He goes to school with my brother, Steven. He's always talking about what a great basketball player Andy is."

Melissa smiled. "Yeah, I guess he's pretty good."

"I had to get some glue for our science project," Amy said. "I hope you two are here for something more exciting than tape and glue."

Jessica saw her chance to get rid of Elizabeth. "We just came by to pick up a couple of things for Mom," Jessica said. She turned to Elizabeth. "I'll go in and get the stuff."

"All right," Elizabeth said. She turned back to Amy and Melissa, and Jessica went inside.

Valley Pharmacy was one of Jessica's favorite stores. It had jewelry, a big cosmetics counter, and a great selection of candy. Jessica could spend hours prowling the aisles. In fact, she had come so often, some of the salespeople knew her by name.

Suddenly Jessica had an idea. She would get the bunch of balloons, and if Elizabeth asked her how she had paid for them, she would say she got them on credit because she knew the sales clerk.

Jessica spotted the balloons in the back of the store and hurried toward them. "I'd like six balloons with hearts on them," she told the clerk.

The clerk tied the bunch together with a ribbon. Then he rang them up on the register. "That will be six forty-five with tax," he said.

Jessica pulled the wad of money from her pocket and began to peel off seven bills. Then she heard a gasp at her elbow. She whirled around and saw Elizabeth staring at the wad.

"Where did you get that money?" Elizabeth hissed.

"Not now," Jessica responded. She didn't want any money arguments in front of the clerk. "Wait until we get outside."

The clerk handed Jessica her change and the bouquet of balloons. "Do you have a big bag?" she asked. "I've got to take these on my bike, and it will be easier if they're not blowing around."

"Sure," he answered. He pulled a large plastic bag from under the counter and gave it to Jessica.

"We just have to do one thing first," Jessica said to Elizabeth. She handed the balloons to her. "We'll tie the letters on now, then we'll put it all in the bag before we leave the store. Amy and Melissa might still be outside. We don't want them to see these and get suspicious."

Elizabeth nodded and tied a gold *K*, *T*, and *N* to the strings. Jessica held the bag and Elizabeth stuffed the helium balloons into it. It made a bulky package, but at least no one would guess what was inside.

As they stepped away from the counter, Elizabeth looked at Jessica, her eyes narrow with suspicion. "OK, where did you get that money, Jessica?"

"I found it," Jessica said, her voice defiant. Jessica grabbed the bag and headed for the door before Elizabeth could ask her any more questions.

It would be just like Elizabeth to make her return the balloons if she found out the truth, Jessica thought. But Jessica was determined to deliver the balloons to Cathy.

Outside, Jessica was thrilled to see that Amy and Melissa were still there. Elizabeth could hardly press her for information with them around.

But Jessica did not stop to speak to them. She just waved and hurried to her bicycle. She unlocked it as quickly as she could, her fingers fumbling with the lock.

Over her shoulder, she could hear Elizabeth telling her friends goodbye. It was a good thing Elizabeth was so polite. No matter how eager she was to grill Jessica, she would never brush past Amy and Melissa the way Jessica had.

Jessica hopped on her bicycle and pedaled off

toward Cathy Connors's house. The extra minutes put her at least a block ahead of Elizabeth.

Jessica reached the corner. As she turned, she looked behind her. Elizabeth was racing after her. "Jessica! Stop!" she said.

Jessica pretended she didn't hear and pedaled harder. Cathy Connors lived just a few houses down.

Jessica guided her bike off the street and onto the sidewalk. She laid it down carefully on the sidewalk next to the high hedge that ran around the Connors's house, so she could not be seen from the house. She kept her head low as she removed the balloons from the plastic bag.

Elizabeth pulled up, panting. "Where did you get that money, Jessica?" She sounded mad now.

"Shh," Jessica hissed, motioning to Elizabeth to get behind the hedge. Elizabeth got off her bike and laid it next to Jessica's. Before she could say another word, Jessica had darted around the hedge with the balloons.

She ran to the front door and quickly tied the balloons to the door handle. She rang the bell and raced back around the hedge to join Elizabeth.

"Jessica!" Elizabeth whispered.

"Shh," Jessica said again. She was peering intently through the hedge. As she watched,

Cathy opened the front door and let out a shriek of happy surprise.

"Come on," Jessica hissed. She grabbed Elizabeth by the hand and yanked her a few yards down the block. Then Jessica turned around, doubled back, and forced Elizabeth to turn with her.

"*What* are we doing?" Elizabeth asked, dizzy from Jessica's maneuvers.

"You'll see," Jessica said. As they walked along the sidewalk, they passed the Connors's front walk. From where Cathy stood, it would look as if they just happened to be strolling by.

Jessica turned and waved. "Hi, Cathy."

Cathy looked up and smiled at the twins. "Hi there," she called out. "Taking a walk?"

"Yeah," Jessica said. "It's such a beautiful day, we decided to go out and enjoy it."

The twins walked up to the front door. "What's with the balloons?" Jessica asked with a grin. "Another present from your secret admirer?"

"Did Steven tell you about that?" Cathy asked eagerly.

"No," said Elizabeth hastily. "We heard it from Caroline Pearce's sister, Anita."

"Oh," Cathy said flatly. Jessica thought she caught a note of disappointment in her voice.

Then Cathy laughed. "Anita Pearce is such a gossip," she said. "I guess she told you about the letters too. Look, here's three more. A *K, T,* and *N.* Hmmmmm. Put that with the others, and it could be . . . hmmmmmm . . . DEKE NATLER!" Cathy clapped her hands. "Deke Natler is pretty cute, actually. I wouldn't mind having him for a secret admirer."

Jessica exchanged a worried look with Elizabeth and made a face. "Yuck!" she exclaimed. "Steven says he's a total geek. He says he wears a tie to school and reads the financial pages of the newspaper." Jessica actually did remember hearing Steven say that.

Cathy sighed. "He does. So I guess he's not really my type. I just wish I knew who my secret admirer was." She gave the twins a searching look. "You're sure Steven hasn't said anything? I mean—he might have heard somebody talking, or something like that."

Both twins gave her their most innocent stare. "No," said Jessica. "He hasn't said anything to me. How about you, Elizabeth?"

Elizabeth shook her head. "No. But then, you know how secretive Steven is."

"He is, isn't he?" Cathy's face brightened. "I mean, it's not easy for him to express how he feels, is it?" Cathy smiled to herself. Then she looked at her watch.

"Oh, no," she said. "I've got to get ready for work."

"We've got to get going too," Jessica said. "Have a good day at work."

Cathy went inside the house and shut the door. Jessica and Elizabeth continued along the walk for a few yards, then ran back to get the bicycles.

Jessica giggled. "It's working. She's really hoping it's Steven. I can't believe how brilliant we are. Those *Staying Up with Bob* tickets are as good as ours."

"Jessica," Elizabeth said impatiently. "Where did you get that money? You might as well tell me because I'm going to keep asking you until you do."

Jessica climbed onto her bike. "Ask me no questions and I'll tell you no lies," she said breezily, and pedaled away.

Eight

◇

Steven was very busy that afternoon at McRobert's. The lunch crowd was just starting to pour in, and he had to serve customers, keep the deep fryer going, and stay as far away from Revolting Rick as possible.

But in spite of being busy, he was having a pretty good time. Cathy had been in a great mood when she came in. They had been joking together all afternoon. The only thing that bothered him was her secret admirer. Apparently, the guy had sent her some balloons that morning.

Steven couldn't quite figure out why it bugged him so much. He had always thought of Cathy as a buddy. But ever since this secret admirer stuff started, there were times when she acted as silly as his sisters.

Steven stood at the register entering orders as the customers placed them. "May I help you?" Steven asked. He carefully kept his attention focused on the register. He'd jammed it twice already that morning, and he didn't want another surly lecture from Revolting Rick.

"I'd like a large burger, medium soda, and an ice cream," answered the customer.

"Would you like fries with that?" Steven asked automatically.

"You bet," the customer said. "And throw in an order of gopher nuggets and lint balls."

Steven looked up and saw Joe Howell grinning at him. "You idiot," Steven said, laughing. "You know we only serve gopher nuggets and lint balls during the breakfast shift."

Joe cracked up. "So how's it going?"

"Unbelievably busy," Steven said as he rang up Joe's order. "That'll be three dollars and fifty-six cents."

Joe handed Steven a five-dollar bill, and Steven gave him the change. "I'll be right back with your food," he told Joe.

Steven grabbed a bag and filled it with Joe's burger, soda, and ice cream. He hurried back to the counter and gave it to him.

Joe was frowning at the money in his hand.

"Hey, Steven," he said. "You gave me too much change. I gave you a five. This is change for a ten." Joe handed Steven back the extra money.

"Thanks, Joe," Steven said gratefully. And he meant it. Revolting Rick had made it plain that if there were any discrepancies in the cash drawer, it would come out of Steven's paycheck. "You know, a lot of people would have just kept it and not said anything."

Joe playfully punched Steven in the arm. "Come on. I wouldn't cheat my best friend."

As Steven watched Joe walk away, his heart plummetted into his stomach. No, Joe wouldn't cheat Steven. But Steven was planning to cheat Joe. And not just out of a few dollars. Steven was planning to steal his girl.

What kind of person am I turning into? Steven thought. His throat tightened. He felt so guilty, he could hardly stand it.

There was only one honorable thing to do— tell Joe what was going on and how he felt. He decided he'd go by Joe's house that night after work. Hopefully, they could get everything out in the open.

"Hey, Wakefield!" Revolting Rick shouted. "Snap to out there. Why are you just standing there staring into space when there are people waiting to eat?"

Steven quickly focused his attention back on his work. There were lots of people in line. Everybody had heard Rick chew him out, and a few people were snickering.

Steven flushed with embarrassment and anger. As he quickly assembled the next order, he felt a soft hand on his arm. "He's just mad because he's got a brand-new zit on his chin," Cathy whispered, a malicious twinkle in her eye. "Must be the fried food."

Steven laughed so hard, he thought his sides would split. He felt immediately cheered. Good old Cathy!

That evening, after work, Steven rang Joe's doorbell.

Joe peeked out the window and broke into a grin as he opened the door. "Steven! Come on in. Did you bring me some gopher nuggets?"

Steven tried to smile. But it came out more like a grimace. This wasn't going to be easy.

"Something wrong?" Joe asked.

"I don't know how to say this, but . . ." Steven struggled to find the right words.

"What is it? You're starting to worry me."

Steven took a deep breath. Then he blurted it out. "It's about Jill. I still really like her. I just thought I should tell you that."

Joe gave Steven a strange look. "That's cool," he said. "Jill's a really—uh, uh . . ."

"Great girl," Steven finished for him. "I know she is. And you're a great guy. That's why I don't want to be a snake and lose you as my best friend."

Joe gave Steven a smile. "Like I said, Steven, it's cool. I don't know quite how to say this without sounding mean, but I don't really like Jill that much. Or at least not as much as she likes me. If you can get her to go out with you, that's fine with me."

Steven was stunned. How could Joe not like a fabulous girl like Jill? Was he crazy?

"Besides," Joe added, "I don't really have much time for girls these days. I'm kind of busy with a new hobby. Come on out to the garage, and I'll show you."

Steven followed Joe through the kitchen and into the garage. Joe snapped on the garage light, and Steven saw something large covered with a dust sheet.

"I've been meaning to tell you about it," Joe

said. "But I wanted to wait until I had it. I wasn't sure I could talk my folks into it."

Joe whipped the dust sheet away, and Steven's stomach lurched. It was a *motorcycle*. Old and rusty—but a motorcycle.

Joe beamed. "She's a junker, but I'm going to work on her after school. My dad used to ride motorcycles when he was in college. He's going to help me out. And there's this really great guy at the newsstand who's given me a lot of good magazines—"

"His name's Pete, right?" Steven interrupted.

Joe looked surprised. "How do you know Pete?"

"Oh, I ran into him once," Steven muttered as he eyed the motorcycle. He could hardly bring himself to ask the question, but he knew he had to. "Does Jill like motorcycles?"

Joe shrugged. "She said she does—but only after I told her I wanted one. Jill always says she likes the things I like. That's why it's hard for me to get really interested in her. I'd rather spend time with a girl that has some ideas of her own—not somebody who just pretends to like everything I do."

Steven felt as if his heart were breaking. "I guess she does that because she really likes you."

Joe looked a little ashamed of himself. "I guess so." He looked at Steven hopefully. "Maybe she'll start liking you instead of me. She says she thinks you're really nice."

Steven shook his head. "Nah. I don't have a chance. It's just like the motorcycle. She says she likes me because *you* like me."

Joe covered the motorcycle back up and tried to change the subject. "Hey, I got some new CDs. You want to make a couple of sandwiches and listen to them?"

"No thanks," Steven said. "I've got some things to do at home. I promised my folks I wouldn't let my job interfere with chores and stuff."

"What made you decide to get a job, anyway?" Joe asked.

Steven sighed. He couldn't possibly explain now. "I don't know. Just seemed like a good idea, I guess."

Joe lifted the garage door a few feet. Steven slipped under it and out into the night. "See you Monday," he heard Joe call.

"Right," Steven answered.

As Steven trudged home, his feet felt as if they weighed twenty pounds each. What was the point of getting a motorcycle now? Jill was not interested in motorcycles. She was only interested in Joe. All his effort had been wasted. He had no chance of winning her.

All he had was a stupid job at a fast-food place, complete with a stupid orange hat. To top it off, if he quit, his parents would hit the roof.

What a mess!

Nine

Jessica buried her head deeper into her pillow. In her dream, someone was calling her name. Couldn't they see she was trying to sleep? She snuggled under the blanket.

"Wake up," the voice said again.

"Nooooo," Jessica muttered into her pillow. She wished the voice would shut up.

The voice became more insistent. "Jessica! Jessica!"

Jessica groaned and opened her eyes.

"Wake up, Jessica!"

It wasn't a dream. It was Elizabeth's voice. But where was it coming from?

Jessica turned over and rubbed her eyes. Then she blinked. She could see Elizabeth standing in the bathroom. She was holding something over the toilet bowl—something small and square.

"Are you awake?" Elizabeth asked gently.

"Now I am," Jessica answered grumpily.

"Good." Elizabeth smiled. She waved the small square object in her hand. "Recognize this?"

Jessica began to sense trouble. "What is it?"

"It's a cassette," Elizabeth said. Her voice was syrupy sweet. "Guess which one."

"Johnny Buck?" Jessica asked.

Elizabeth gave Jessica a wide smile. "That's right!"

Then abruptly, her brows snapped together, and she gave her twin a steely glare. Her voice became determined and threatening. "For the eighty-seventh time—*where did you get the money?* Tell me, or Johnny Buck takes a dive!"

Jessica's eyes narrowed. "You wouldn't dare."

Elizabeth's jaw jutted forward. She flushed the toilet and dangled the cassette over the bowl. "Oh, yes I would," she said through clenched teeth.

Jessica eyed her sister, sizing her up. She looked serious, all right—serious enough to flush Johnny Buck down the toilet. "I found it in the washing machine when I did Steven's laundry," she reluctantly admitted.

"*You mean it's Steven's money!*" Elizabeth shouted. "Are you out of your mind? He'll murder us!"

"No, he won't," Jessica argued. "Remember Mom's finders keepers policy? I found the money in the washer. That means it's mine."

Elizabeth came into Jessica's room and sat on Jessica's bed. "Policy or no policy, you have to put it back."

Jessica snatched the cassette and put it under her pillow, safely out of Elizabeth's reach. "No way! I found the money fair and square. Besides, we're using it for Steven's own good."

"*We* are not using the money for anything," Elizabeth said, "because *I* don't want to have anything to do with it. Put the money back in Steven's room, or count me out of the project."

"Fine," Jessica replied. "I'll just have to keep going without you. You're not the only one who can cut letters out of cardboard, you know."

"That's true. But I know which letters we've sent and which letters we haven't. Do you?"

Jessica frowned. Elizabeth had a point. Jessica hadn't really paid much attention to the letters. She had left that part to Elizabeth. "If I give it a little thought, I'm sure I'll figure it out," she bluffed.

"Fine," Elizabeth said. "Then you won't need me—or my camera."

"Elizabeth," Jessica wheedled, "I need the camera to get proof for Janet."

"If you give it a little thought," Elizabeth said sweetly, "I'm sure you'll figure something out."

"Don't you want to see *Staying Up with Bob*?" Jessica demanded.

"No!" Elizabeth shouted. "As far as I'm concerned, 'Project Get Rid of Jill' is finished." Elizabeth stalked into the bathroom and slammed the door.

Sunday breakfast was a silent meal. Elizabeth and Jessica weren't speaking. Steven seemed too gloomy and preoccupied to talk. And Mr. Wakefield had eaten early and gone into his den to catch up on some paperwork.

"How was work yesterday, Steven?" Mrs. Wakefield asked, finally breaking the silence.

"OK," Steven mumbled, reaching for the syrup for his pancakes. As Jessica watched, he poured syrup over his eggs.

Jessica caught Elizabeth's eye and gave a little flick of her head. Elizabeth looked over at Steven just in time to see him reach for the ketchup and pour it all over his pancakes.

The twins watched in amazement as Steven picked up his fork and began to eat. He took one bite after the other, staring glumly into space as he chewed. He didn't even notice that his pancakes were covered with ketchup and his eggs were covered with syrup.

Jessica's heart sank. Steven had almost seemed like his old self the last couple of days. Today he was definitely showing signs of a relapse of Jill Hale-itis.

Elizabeth refused to meet Jessica's eye again. She finished her breakfast in silence and left the table. Jessica hurried after her, catching up with her on the stairs.

"See how bad Steven's gotten?" she whispered. "Are you really going to let him keep suffering like that?"

"He'll get over it," Elizabeth replied coldly. Then she went into her room and shut the door with a bang.

Jessica went into her own room. What was she going to do? She really *couldn't* remember which letters were left to send. Even if she could, what was the point of continuing on her own? Without Elizabeth's camera, there would be no way of getting the proof she needed to win the bet.

Jessica chewed on her nails, thinking hard. Right now, Elizabeth was angry. But Elizabeth could never stay mad at Jessica for long. Once she cooled off, she would change her mind. Jessica began to relax. By this afternoon, Elizabeth would be ready to listen to reason, and "Project Get Rid of Jill" would be back on track.

Jessica had underestimated Elizabeth. All Sunday afternoon, Elizabeth stubbornly refused to have anything to do with her. In fact, she spent most of the day at Amy Sutton's house and talking on the phone to Todd Wilkins. And the last thing she said to Jessica before she went to bed was, "Don't talk to me until you're ready to put the money back."

By Monday afternoon, Jessica realized Elizabeth was one hundred percent serious. She was so frustrated. They had been so close to succeeding! Now they were going to lose the bet and blow their only chance of seeing *Staying Up with Bob*.

At lunchtime, Jessica took her tray to the Unicorner, the special table where all the Unicorns sat. Janet Howell gave her a nasty smile. "In case you've forgotten, Jessica, tomorrow is the day you're supposed to prove that Steven is over Jill Hale. Tomorrow by four o'clock."

"I haven't forgotten," Jessica said.

"You don't think you're actually going to win, do you?"

Jessica ignored the question. She wasn't going to give Janet the satisfaction of looking worried.

"By the way, what kind of film does that camera take? I can't wait to start taking pictures with it."

The other Unicorns laughed, and Jessica's mouth suddenly went dry. To Jessica, losing the bet had meant losing the *Staying Up with Bob* tickets. She had forgotten that it meant losing the camera too.

The way Elizabeth was acting, Jessica wasn't even sure that she would give up the camera if they lost. And if Jessica couldn't deliver the camera, she'd be a *welcher*—something no Unicorn had ever been. They might even throw her out of the club.

Jessica's mind raced. Technically, Elizabeth had been involved in the bet too. So *technically*, Elizabeth had just as much of an obligation as Jessica did.

On the other hand, it was Jessica who had proposed the bet. And she had done it without asking Elizabeth's permission. So it would be Jessica's responsibility to pay up if it came to that. And it was Jessica that the others would blame if she couldn't.

There was no way around it. She was going to have to give in to Elizabeth. And she was going to have to do it soon. Time was running out.

Jessica worked hard to keep her face from betraying her feelings. She turned to Janet and smiled. "I wouldn't buy any film yet." She stood up. "I'll see you tomorrow."

Jessica got rid of her tray and looked around for Elizabeth. She spotted her sitting on the other side of the cafeteria with Amy Sutton. Jessica hurried over to their table and tapped Elizabeth on the shoulder. "Can I talk to you for a minute?"

Elizabeth looked at her coldly. "What about?"

Jessica looked at Amy. She was watching the twins with curiosity.

"Could we talk about it privately?" Jessica begged.

"I'm a little busy right now," Elizabeth replied.

"Please, Elizabeth! It's important."

Elizabeth turned to Amy. "Would you mind?"

"No, go ahead," Amy said, trying hard not to laugh. Usually, it was Jessica who had Elizabeth at the disadvantage.

Elizabeth got up and followed Jessica to an empty table. "You win." Jessica sighed. "I can't go on with 'Project Get Rid of Jill' without you. I'll put the money back."

Elizabeth smiled. "Promise?"

"Promise."

Elizabeth reached over and gave Jessica's arm a squeeze. Jessica immediately felt better. She really didn't like being in a fight with her twin.

Elizabeth pointed to her bag. "I knew you'd come around. So I've got everything we need with me. We don't have much time left, so we'd better send all the rest of the letters today."

"But what are we going to do about a present?"

"We'll just have to send them without a present. It may be cheap," Elizabeth said, looking thoughtful, "but then again . . . Steven *is* kind of cheap."

Jessica giggled. Elizabeth giggled too. Soon they were both laughing so hard that tears were running down their cheeks. They laughed so hard that the kids at the next table looked over to see what was going on.

"What's the joke?" asked Rick Hunter, a handsome eighth grader.

Neither Jessica nor Elizabeth could speak. All they could do was laugh.

"Guess you have to be a Wakefield twin to get it," said Bruce Patman, another eighth-grade boy.

Normally, Jessica would have been thrilled that the boys had noticed her. But today, she was just happy to be sharing a joke with her sister.

Ten

◇

That afternoon at McRobert's, Steven was so depressed, he could hardly stand up straight. It was impossible to keep his mind on his work. All he could think about was Jill and what a jerk he had been. He made all kinds of stupid mistakes at work, like jamming the cash register and giving people the wrong food.

Revolting Rick had yelled at him three times—twice in front of customers. And one of the customers had been Andy McCormick.

Andy was a senior and maybe the best player on the varsity basketball team. He had stopped by for some food, and he and Steven had started talking about basketball.

Andy had been giving him some really good tips when Revolting Rick interrupted and told Steven he wasn't paying him to gossip with his little school friend. Steven could have punched him. Steven's "little school friend" could mop up the court with a creep like Rick. Luckily, Andy hadn't taken offense. He just gave Steven a grin and a thumbs-up sign and headed out the door.

"Hey, Wakefield!" Revolting Rick shouted as Steven put fries into the deep fryer.

Steven looked up. Rick was shutting the door of his office and straightening his tie. "I'm gonna slip out for a while and pay a little visit to the main squeeze—know what I mean?" Rick winked.

He really thinks he's cool, Steven thought in amazement. *What a geek!*

"You and Connors try not to burn the place down while I'm gone," Rick added with a sneer.

Steven nodded and shoved a bunch of buns into the warmer. Now he felt even more depressed. Even a repulsive nerd like Rick had better luck with girls than he did.

As depressed as he was, Steven felt relieved as he watched Rick disappear into the mall. At least he'd be off Steven's back for a little while.

"Steven!" he heard Cathy shriek.

Steven turned and saw Cathy running toward the deep fryer. Black smoke was pouring out of it. He had forgotten about the French fries.

Cathy carefully turned off the fryer and lifted the fries out. They were burnt to a crisp. She dumped a fresh load of fries into the vat and sighed unhappily.

"I'm sorry, Cathy," Steven said.

Cathy didn't say anything. She just sighed again and turned back to the cash register.

"I really am sorry, Cathy. It won't happen again, I promise. Please don't be mad at me."

Cathy looked up at Steven in surprise. "Don't be ridiculous. Why would I be mad at you?"

"For burning the fries," Steven answered.

"Who cares about the stupid French fries?" Cathy asked. She sounded irritable.

Steven looked at her closely. Something was definitely bothering her. Now that he thought about it, she hadn't been her usual self all afternoon.

"Is Rick getting you down?" he asked gently.

Cathy shook her head. "That's not what's bothering me."

"Well, what *is* bothering you?" Steven asked.

Cathy seemed reluctant to answer at first. Then she gave Steven a long look. "I haven't heard from my secret admirer since Saturday," she said. "I'm afraid he's lost interest."

Steven knew just how Cathy felt. He patted her shoulder sympathetically. "Looks like we're both unlucky in love," he said.

Cathy frowned. "What do you mean?"

Steven sighed. "I mean that the only reason I got this job was so I could buy a motorcycle to impress Jill Hale. Now it turns out that she couldn't care less about motorcycles—or me."

Cathy gave Steven a curious smile. "You like Jill Hale?"

Steven nodded.

"I didn't realize that," Cathy said softly. "Some friend I am, huh? You must think I'm pretty dumb."

"You're a great friend," Steven protested. "It's me that's dumb—mooning over a girl who hates me. I took her out on probably the worst date in history, and now I act like a jerk every time I get near her."

"Why would she hate you?" Cathy asked. "You're a great guy. I'm sure if you just relaxed and acted like yourself around her, she'd go out with you. Any girl would—unless she's completely stupid. And Jill's not stupid."

Steven shook his head. "Thanks for the pep talk, coach. But this player is out of the game."

Cathy put her hands on her hips and glared at Steven. "All right then, here's another approach. Cheer up—or else!"

Cathy picked up a frozen French fry and dropped it down the back of his shirt.

Steven yelped as he removed the frozen fry. "You're dead, Connors," he said, laughing.

Steven reached for a handful of the fries. He threw them at Cathy as she laughingly ducked behind a condiment counter.

Before Steven could react, she scooped up a fistful of shredded lettuce and threw it at him.

"Bull's-eye!" Cathy giggled as the lettuce landed squarely on Steven's head and draped over the brim of his hat. Cathy grabbed a handful of tomatoes and prepared to launch a second attack.

But Steven saw it coming. He grabbed a strawberry shake from the counter and lunged at Cathy before she could throw it. As he did, he slammed into the condiment counter, and the whole thing crashed to the ground.

Lettuce, pickles, tomatoes, and onions flew in every direction, covering the floor and splattering Steven and Cathy.

"Oh!" Steven gasped in horror. Then he began to laugh so hard, he doubled over.

Cathy, who was laughing almost as hard,

leaped at the opportunity. She grabbed the shake from Steven's hand and, before he could duck, poured it all over him. Thick strawberry goo ran down Steven's shirt.

Steven wiped off a big gob of it with his hand and lobbed it in Cathy's direction.

The strawberry mess hit Cathy in the eye. Giggling, she took a step toward the paper towels. As she did, she slid on a tomato, going down hard on her bottom in the middle of a bed of pickles and onions. "Yuck!" she shrieked.

Steven waded through the mess to help Cathy up. "Are you all right?" he managed to say between gasps of laughter.

Cathy nodded, laughing as she struggled to her feet.

"Excuse me," said a voice at the counter.

Cathy and Steven jumped guiltily apart and looked toward the counter. Steven's heart gave a thud. *It was Jill Hale!*

Neither Steven nor Cathy was laughing now. For a stunned moment, all they could do was stare at Jill, open-mouthed.

Cathy came to her senses first. "Ask her out now," she hissed, pushing Steven toward the counter.

With his heart pounding, Steven gave Jill a

smile. "Hi, Jill," he said. His voice sounded thin and high. He cleared his throat, trying to get it back to its normal pitch. "What would you like?"

Jill gave him a tight smile. "I'll have a fish sandwich to go. That's a dollar eighty-nine, right? I've got it exactly." She pulled the money out of her purse and placed it on the counter, carefully avoiding Steven's sticky hand.

Steven put the money in the drawer and hurried to get the sandwich.

Cathy had grabbed a broom and was pretending to sweep up in the back. When Steven looked up at her, she made an encouraging face. "Ask her out," she mouthed.

Steven shook his head. "No."

"Chicken," Cathy hissed.

Steven was stunned. Cathy had called him lots of things. But never chicken. All right, then. He'd show her.

Steven took the bag to the counter. "Say, uh, Jill," he began. "I know our last date didn't work out too well, but would you like to go out with me again . . . to a movie?"

Steven held his breath, waiting for Jill to answer. She gave him a long look that seemed to take in the lettuce hanging from the brim of his

hat and the strawberry goo that soaked the front
of his brown-and-orange polyester shirt.

Jill's mouth opened and she burst out laughing. "Oh, Steven—you're such a comedian."

She picked up her bag, still laughing, and
walked out of McRobert's.

Steven stood there, stunned. He couldn't
believe it. Cathy came over and stood by his side.

"She didn't even bother to say no," he said
woefully. "She just acted like it was a big joke."
Steven had never felt so humiliated in his whole
life.

"I guess she *is* stupid, after all," Cathy said.
"Who'd pass up a chance to go out with you?
You're a great guy—even though your personal
hygiene stinks." Cathy flicked a piece of lettuce
from the brim of Steven's hat.

Steven smiled. Then he began to laugh. Cathy
laughed too. Soon they were laughing so hard,
they could hardly stand. They had to hold each
other up to keep from slipping on the tomatoes,
lettuce, pickles, and onions that covered the floor.

Steven reached over and wiped a spot of
strawberry shake off of Cathy's face. Funny how
he'd never noticed how pretty she was—even
with that gook on her face.

As he wiped her cheek, Steven realized that he wasn't laughing anymore. And neither was Cathy.

He took a step closer. Suddenly, he felt very confused. More than anything else, he wanted to kiss Cathy. But how could that be? Cathy was just a friend—wasn't she?"

" 'Scuse me."

Again, Cathy and Steven jumped guiltily apart. A little boy stood at the counter.

Cathy sighed. "I'll take care of him."

"I'll get the mop and start cleaning up," Steven mumbled. He grabbed the mop, his mind in a whirl. *It's almost like I have a crush on Cathy*, he thought to himself. *But is it really a crush?*

Steven didn't know what to think. The way he was feeling about Cathy wasn't at all the way he had felt about Jill. Whenever he thought about Jill, he felt sick to his stomach, nervous, and unhappy. Thinking about Cathy made him feel happy.

But then Steven realized that people who like each other are supposed to feel happy. Of course! So what if Cathy was a friend? She could be a girlfriend too.

Steven felt as if he could fly. In a second, all the unhappiness of the last few weeks was forgotten. Steven looked over at Cathy, eager to tell her how he felt.

He watched as Cathy went over to the counter to take the little boy's order. But the little boy didn't want to order any food. Instead, he held out an envelope. "This is for you," he said.

Cathy took the envelope. "Who gave you this?" she asked.

The little boy smiled and shook his head. "Can't tell." He giggled and ran out.

Cathy opened the envelope and removed a gold *V, W, A, S, F,* and *I.*

Steven walked over and watched as Cathy spread the letters out on the counter. His heart began to ache. "Your secret admirer?" he asked.

Cathy nodded. She reached under the counter and pulled all the other letters out of her bag. She began moving them around on the counter, trying to make them spell a name.

Wouldn't you know it? Steven thought. *Here I am, crazy about Cathy, and it's too late. Some other guy's already won her over with this secret admirer stuff.*

"KEVIN ALSTEAD . . . no . . . LEE WAST-FELD . . . no." Cathy's fingers quickly moved the last two letters into place. All together, they spelled . . . STEVEN WAKEFIELD!

Steven gasped in surprise, and Cathy gave a shout of glee. "You didn't do this, did you?"

Steven shook his head ruefully. "No. But I would have if I'd had any brains at all."

Cathy's eyes gleamed with amusement. "What about Jill?"

"Jill who?"

Cathy turned her face up and laughed. Steven seized his opportunity. He bent down and kissed her lips. And as he did, a bright light flashed.

Once again, Steven and Cathy jumped apart. They blinked as spots danced in their eyes. *That was some kiss!* Steven thought. He suddenly heard a familiar squeal.

"We did it! We did it!"

Steven looked up and saw Elizabeth and Jessica jumping up and down in excitement. Elizabeth was holding her camera.

Cathy laughed and waved a couple of letters. "I take it you two sent these?"

"That's right," Jessica said proudly. "We knew you two were right for each other, so we came up with a plan to get you together. And it worked. Just like on *Days of Turmoil.*"

"Speaking of turmoil," Steven said. He pointed to the door.

Everyone turned and saw Revolting Rick

standing in the doorway, surveying the damage. "You're both fired," he snarled.

Steven looked at Cathy. Cathy looked at Steven. Then they both threw their orange hats into the air and shouted, *"Hooray!"*

Eleven

◇

Much to Steven's surprise, Mr. and Mrs. Wakefield were not angry over his dismissal. They said it was just as well. Steven had more than enough to do between schoolwork and extracurricular activities.

And they thought the story of Cathy's "secret admirer" was very funny. "I don't know what made you girls take such an interest in your brother's love life," Mr. Wakefield said, "but you seem to have brought things to a happy conclusion."

Elizabeth and Jessica had decided not to tell them about the bet and *Staying Up with Bob* until things had settled down a little.

"I must say it's nice to have Steven back to his old self," Mrs. Wakefield said at the dinner table that night.

"He actually speaks when he's spoken to," added Mr. Wakefield. "A definite improvement."

"And he's not soaked in that awful cologne," Jessica pointed out. "If it hadn't been for us playing Cupid," she went on, eager to claim credit for herself and Elizabeth, "Steven would still be walking around like a zombie, and he and Cathy would never have gotten together."

Steven grinned. "Don't think that I'm not grateful," he said, helping himself to more peas. "But from now on, stay out of my love life. I don't need any more help from you two."

"I don't know about that," Elizabeth teased. "It looks to me like you need all the help you can get."

"Oh, yeah?" Steven picked up a pea and playfully threw it across the table at Elizabeth.

Elizabeth quickly angled her knife and batted the pea back across the table, where it hit Steven squarely on the forehead.

Everyone, including Elizabeth, was astonished.

"Bet you can't do that again," Steven challenged.

Elizabeth angled her knife. "You're on."

Steven tossed another pea at Elizabeth. Again, she caught the pea with the end of her knife and batted it back toward Steven. The pea smacked him right in the middle of his forehead.

Steven laughed so hard, he choked on a piece of bread. Then, hoping to take her by surprise, he quickly tossed another pea.

Elizabeth still managed to bat the pea back to Steven and hit him in the exact same place.

By then, the whole family was laughing. "It's like she can't miss!" Steven exclaimed.

Mrs. Wakefield laughed. "I can see you have real talent, Elizabeth. But no more stunts at the table, please."

"*Stunts!*" shouted Jessica and Elizabeth together.

"*That's it!*" Jessica yelled. "That's a really stupid stunt! Now you can go on the show!"

Elizabeth was thrilled.

Then she noticed that her parents and Steven were looking at them curiously.

"What show?" Steven asked.

Elizabeth looked at Jessica. The cat was out of the bag now. "Well," she began uneasily. "The reason we decided to get involved in Steven's uh . . . problem—is . . . uh . . . uh—"

Mr. Wakefield sighed. "I had a feeling there was more to this than met the eye. 'Fess up, girls.

What's the story?" He looked at Jessica significantly. "The *true* story." His tone was pleasant, but the twins could tell he meant business.

"We had a bet with Janet Howell," Jessica explained. "If we could prove that Steven wasn't interested in Jill Hale anymore, then she would give us her two tickets to the *Staying Up with Bob* show in Los Angeles."

Steven buried his face in his hands. "You mean everybody in town has been talking about my love life?" He groaned.

"Not everybody," Jessica corrected. "Just the Unicorns."

Steven groaned again.

Mr. Wakefield frowned. "And if you lost the bet, what were you going to give Janet?"

Elizabeth hesitated. She knew he wasn't going to like the answer. "My camera," she admitted.

"Look girls," Mr. Wakefield said, "a friendly bet is one thing. But when it gets to the point where you kids are betting expensive items like cameras and show tickets, it's gone too far."

"I'm sorry, Dad," Elizabeth said quietly.

"I'm sure the Howells would feel the same way," added Mrs. Wakefield. "I know that Janet bet her tickets in good faith. But I just don't feel that it's appropriate for you girls to take them from her."

Elizabeth and Jessica looked at each other in shock. "You mean we can't go to *Staying Up with Bob*?" Jessica asked, on the verge of tears. "All that hard work for nothing?"

Mr. Wakefield raised his brows. "I wouldn't call your brother's happiness 'nothing,' would you?"

"What if they bought the tickets from Janet?" Steven asked.

The twins looked at Steven in amazement. "What?"

"I guess I do owe them something for their trouble. If Janet will sell them the tickets, I'll pay for them. I've heard from other kids that they're fifteen dollars, and I've got thirty dollars in my bank."

"Actually, you have twenty-four dollars and sixty-seven cents," Jessica said quickly. "I found your sock—I mean your bank—in the washing machine when I did your laundry. I used some of it to pay for Cathy's balloons. The rest I put back in your room—even though technically it's mine."

Steven let out an outraged grunt. He struggled to find words to express his anger.

Elizabeth and Jessica stared at him across the table, their eyes wide and innocent.

"You're not *mad*, are you?" Jessica asked, pretending to be surprised.

Steven's face collapsed, and his shoulders shook as anger gave way to silent laughter. All he could do was shake his head and wheeze.

Elizabeth and Jessica continued to stare.

Finally, Steven was able to talk. "The man at the swim club—he said you two must make life *interesting*."

Mrs. Wakefield passed a plate of roast beef toward the twins. "I think that what your brother is trying to say is that he considers that a masterpiece of understatement."

Steven nodded, still gasping with laughter.

"Does your offer still stand, Steven?" Mr. Wakefield asked with a grin.

Steven nodded and wiped his eyes. "Sure."

Mr. Wakefield seemed thoughtful for a minute. "All right, then. If Janet will sell you the tickets for thirty dollars, I'll make up the difference and play chauffeur to Los Angeles—but only on the condition that you two get a grip on this gambling fever." He laughed. "I don't want to come home one day and discover that you've lost the house in a bet involving the correct spelling of Johnny Buck's mother's maiden name."

The twins laughed.

"Thanks, Steven. Thanks, Dad," Elizabeth said, her eyes sparkling. She couldn't remember the last time she'd felt so happy.

From here on, it was smooth sailing. All she and Jessica had to do now was get the picture to Janet by four o'clock tomorrow afternoon.

The next day at lunch, Jessica sat down at the Unicorner with her tray. "Hello, Jessica," Janet said.

"Hi," Jessica said, opening her milk.

The other Unicorns stared at Jessica, obviously eager to know the outcome of the bet. But Jessica had decided to make things as dramatic as possible.

"Well?" Kimberly asked.

"Well what?" Jessica responded.

"Did you win the bet?" Tamara asked.

Jessica smiled mischievously. "Meet me at Janet's house at four o'clock. You'll all find out then."

*   *   *

After school, Elizabeth raced to the drugstore. She had deposited her film the evening before in the night-deposit box. She prayed that the film would be developed and that the picture had come out clearly.

Elizabeth rushed inside. Fortunately, the pictures were ready. Her hands were shaking as she opened the package. What if the pictures hadn't come out? What if she had used too much flash? What if she hadn't used enough?

Elizabeth didn't need to worry. She was a born photographer, and she grinned when she saw the print. She had captured Cathy and Steven's first kiss perfectly.

She looked at her watch. She had only twenty minutes to get to Janet's house.

Elizabeth hopped on her bicycle and began to pedal as fast as she could. But as she approached the avenue leading to Janet's neighborhood, she saw a big truck blocking her way. A team of workmen were tearing up the street, and water was spewing out of a gutter. A man holding a red flag signaled Elizabeth to stop. "I'm sorry, miss," he said. "There was a break in one of the water pipes under the street. This whole side of the neighborhood is blocked off. You'll have to detour around Elm Avenue."

"But that will take forever," Elizabeth objected. "Can't I just walk my bike through the construction?"

"I'm sorry," said the man. "I can't allow anyone into this area."

Elizabeth hopped back on her bike and pedaled furiously. It was a long detour. What if she didn't make it in time?

Meanwhile, at Janet's house, the Unicorns were breathless with excitement and suspense. It was almost four o'clock.

Janet tapped her foot impatiently. "I don't know why you're stalling, Jessica. If you have some reason to think Steven is over Jill Hale, why don't you say so? I think you're just wasting our time."

"I still have five minutes," Jessica replied calmly. But inside, she was worried. Where was Elizabeth?

"This is so typical of you, Jess," Lila Fowler said. "You just want to be the center of attention for as long as possible. If you had any proof, you would have told us already."

Jessica just tossed her hair over her shoulder. She couldn't wait to see Lila's face when Elizabeth arrived with the picture.

But would Elizabeth arrive in time? As the

minutes pased, Jessica felt beads of sweat forming on her brow. What was keeping her?

In the hallway, the grandfather clock began to chime the hour: "Bong! . . . Bong! . . . Bong! . . ."

Janet smiled. "Time's up. You just lost your—" She broke off when she heard the front door fly open.

Elizabeth raced into the living room just as the clock struck its last bong. She hadn't even bothered to ring the bell or shut the door behind her. She just ran in, red-faced and breathless. Jessica had to smile. This was very un-Elizabeth-like behavior.

Elizabeth flashed Jessica a grin as she handed the picture to Janet. "Photographic evidence!" she announced triumphantly.

Janet stared at the photo. Her face flushed first with embarrassment, then with anger.

The other Unicorns gathered around, looking at the picture over her shoulder. There was a long silence. Finally Tamara spoke. "I'd say this pretty much proves that Steven is over Jill Hale."

The others nodded solemnly, looking at Janet. Janet was in an ugly mood. Jessica could tell what they were thinking. Tickets or no tickets, none of them would want to be in Jessica's shoes right now.

Janet put the picture down on the table and gave Jessica and Elizabeth a tight smile. "You win," she said shortly. "You get the *Staying Up with Bob* tickets."

Jessica reached into her pocket. "Elizabeth and I talked it over," she said. "And we decided that we want to pay you for the tickets."

She and Elizabeth had decided not to mention, however, that their parents had found out about the bet and insisted that they pay.

Jessica put thirty dollars on the table. But Janet shook her head. "A deal's a deal," she said. "You won the tickets. They're yours. You don't have to pay for them."

"I know," Jessica agreed. "But I think that maybe our gambling is getting out of hand. A friendly bet is one thing. But when it gets to the point where we're betting expensive things like cameras and show tickets, it's going too far."

Jessica ignored the snort of laughter that came from her twin. "I really wouldn't feel right about taking the tickets unless you let me pay for them."

Janet looked thoughtful. "You know, Jessica," she said in her club president voice, "that's very mature of you. I think you're absolutely right. As a favor to you, I will accept the thirty dollars."

Jessica felt a sense of relief. Now Janet could lose the bet without losing face. That meant she wouldn't spend the next few weeks making Jessica's life miserable.

"Let's go upstairs and have our meeting," Janet said. "We can discuss new rules regarding Unicorn bets."

"I'll be up in a minute," Jessica said as all the Unicorns ran upstairs.

"What took you so long?" Jessica asked when she and Elizabeth were alone.

Elizabeth collapsed in a chair. "The streets on the south side were blocked off for construction. I had to detour, and I almost didn't make it."

Jessica smiled. "Well, you did. Just in the nick of time too."

"Jessica," Janet called from upstairs, "are you coming?"

"Go on," Elizabeth said. "I'm just going to sit here for a minute and catch my breath."

Jessica gave her sister a hug and ran up the stairs.

Elizabeth sat alone in the chair. Her heart was still racing from her frantic bicycle ride.

"Hello?" She heard a voice at the door.

Elizabeth looked up as Jill Hale stepped into the living room.

"Hi," Jill said. "The door was open, so I just came in."

"Oh, that was my fault," Elizabeth said. "I forgot to close it. By the way, I'm Elizabeth Wakefield."

"Right—you're Steven's sister."

Elizabeth nodded.

"I was supposed to meet Joe here at four-thirty," Jill explained. "Have you seen him?"

"No," Elizabeth replied. "But it's only four-fifteen. Janet and the Unicorns are upstairs if you feel like going up."

"No, I'll just wait down here," Jill said, walking idly around the room. As she did, her glance fell on the photograph that Janet had left on the table. Jill picked it up and examined it.

"This is a cute picture," she remarked. "I didn't know that Steven and Cathy were, uh . . . a couple."

"It's a pretty recent development," Elizabeth said. She got up from her chair. "I'd better get going. See you."

Jill gave Elizabeth a dazzling smile. "Be sure and tell Steven hello," she said.

Later that night, Elizabeth and Jessica walked into the living room and discovered Steven rolling on the floor with laughter. "Guess who just called," he said. "Take a wild guess."

"Cathy?" Elizabeth guessed.

"No. *Jill Hale!* She wanted to know if I wanted to get together tomorrow night to study."

Jessica's jaw dropped. "What did you tell her?"

"I told her I had other plans." Steven laughed, standing up. "I'm not interested in spending time with Jill Hale anymore. Especially after the way she treated me. I wonder why she called."

"She did see the picture I took of you and Cathy at Janet's house today," Elizabeth admitted. "Maybe that has something to do with it."

Elizabeth was afraid Steven would be angry. But to her surprise, he just looked thoughtful.

"That explains it," he said. "I guess she's just one of those girls who always wants the guy she can't have." Steven walked out of the room shaking his head.

"You see, Elizabeth," Jessica said seriously. "It's exactly like *Days of Turmoil*. Now *that's* what I call educational TV."

Twelve

Jessica and Elizabeth were seated in the studio audience of *Staying Up with Bob*. Mr. Wakefield had driven them into Los Angeles and treated them to dinner before the show. "Break a leg, girls," he'd said as he dropped them off at the studio.

All the audience members who wanted to perform stupid stunts had been asked to sign up prior to the show. They had been given a card that asked for their name and occupation. It also asked them to list any props they might need.

Elizabeth had carefully filled out her card and handed it back to the usher. She had asked for some props, but she had brought her own bag of peas and a knife in case her name was called.

She knew all the kids at Sweet Valley Middle

School would be watching the show tonight, hoping to see her and Jessica. Elizabeth was glad that it was a Friday night so everybody could stay up late and watch.

Lila Fowler had promised to tape the show on her VCR. That way, if they got chosen to perform, the twins could watch themselves later. Elizabeth prayed she would get chosen to perform her stupid stunt.

Bob was especially funny that night. The audience laughed and applauded at all his jokes, and the band played lots of the twins' favorite songs.

Finally Bob announced it was time for "Stupid Stunts." "Our first performer will be"—there was a drum roll, and Elizabeth squeezed her eyes shut, wishing hard—"Elizabeth Wakefield! Assisted by her sister Jessica!" Bob shouted.

"That's us!" Jessica squealed. "Come on, Elizabeth. Come on!"

Elizabeth's hands were shaking as she shoved the bag of peas into Jessica's hand. They ran down the aisle and up onto the stage.

Bob looked from Elizabeth to Jessica and back again. "Identical twins!" he exclaimed. "Two for the price of one!"

The audience laughed as Bob shook their

hands. "Now, which of you is Elizabeth and which is Jessica?" Bob asked.

"I'm Elizabeth," Elizabeth said into the microphone.

"And I'm Jessica."

"And you're both students at Sweet Valley Middle School?"

The twins nodded.

"I understand you asked for some props. We have a very big prop room, so we were able to provide everything. It's all set up." Bob beckoned to a stagehand and a curtain went up, revealing a Ping-Pong table. Just as Elizabeth had requested, the Ping-Pong table had been set like a dinner table with plates, silverware, napkins, and glasses.

The audience giggled. It was a funny prop, but it didn't give the stunt away.

"Can you tell us what we are going to see?" Bob asked.

"Pea-Pong," Elizabeth answered.

"Sort of like dinner-table tennis?" Bob asked with a grin.

"Right," Elizabeth said.

"Well, have a seat, and let the games begin," Bob said.

The audience applauded as Elizabeth and Jessica sat down on either side of the table.

Jessica poured the peas onto her plate, and Elizabeth picked up her knife.

"Shall I serve?" Jessica asked in a very prim and proper voice.

"Oh, yes," Elizabeth answered in the same voice. "Please do."

Jessica flicked a pea at Elizabeth. Elizabeth angled her knife and batted it back at Jessica, hitting her smack in the middle of her forehead.

The audience roared with laughter. Elizabeth looked over and saw that the bandleader was laughing too. He signaled to the drummer. Elizabeth could see he was catching on.

When Jessica picked up the next pea, the drummer obliged with a drum roll. Jessica threw the pea, and when Elizabeth batted it back, the drummer hit the cymbal.

The audience laughed even harder.

Elizabeth and Jessica had been practicing the stunt for days, and they had worked out a routine. Jessica would pretend to get angrier and angrier as she threw the peas, and Elizabeth would pretend not to notice.

Jessica threw pea after pea from every angle, and Elizabeth hit every one of them back across the table, where they smacked Jessica in the forehead, the cheek, and the eye.

The audience was howling with laughter, and Elizabeth was having a hard time not laughing herself. Jessica was covered with peas—they were caught in her hair and stuck to her blouse.

Finally Jessica was left with one last pea on her plate. She flicked it at Elizabeth. This time, instead of hitting it back, Elizabeth ducked her head and caught the pea in her mouth.

"Ta-da," the band played.

The audience jumped to its feet. Elizabeth's heart was pounding as she stood up to take a bow. She grabbed Jessica's hand and they bowed together. The audience was screaming with laughter. *"Pea-Pong . . . Pea-Pong . . . Pea Pong!"* they chanted.

Bob ran over and grabbed Elizabeth's arm, lifting it high in the air. "Ladies and gentlemen, the reigning Pea-Pong champion of California, Miss Elizabeth Wakefield!"

Elizabeth felt tears well up in her eyes. She felt this was probably the best night of her life.

By Monday, when Elizabeth got to school, she and Jessica had become celebrities. Everybody had seen them on *Staying Up with Bob,* and everybody was talking about how great they were.

"You guys put Sweet Valley on the map," Aaron Dallas said proudly before homeroom.

Even Janet Howell had been complimentary. "I probably couldn't have done better myself," she told Elizabeth.

But the real surprise came at lunchtime. When Elizabeth and Jessica walked into the cafeteria, they were greeted with a shower of peas. Everyone in the lunchroom was standing on their chairs tossing peas at them. "Pea-Pong . . . Pea-Pong . . . Pea-Pong!" they chanted.

Laughing, Elizabeth lifted her notebook to shield herself.

Todd Wilkins stepped forward carrying two bouquets of flowers. "To the reigning Pea-Pong champion of California," he said, handing Elizabeth a bouquet.

"Thank you," Elizabeth said, blushing.

"And for her lovely assistant." He handed the other bouquet to Jessica.

Jessica accepted the flowers with a laugh. The cafeteria applauded them.

Elizabeth caught Jessica's eye and smiled. When they worked together, they made a pretty good team.

*   *   *

That afternoon, when Elizabeth stopped by the Dairi Burger to meet Todd, she saw Steven and Cathy sitting at the counter.

"How was school?" Steven asked. "Did anybody see you on television?"

"Everybody saw us," Elizabeth said with a laugh. "We got pelted with peas during lunch."

"Fame has its price," Steven said.

"Everybody at Sweet Valley High saw you too," Cathy said. "You guys were great."

"Hey, there's Andy McCormick," Steven said. "Andy!" he called.

Andy saw Steven and smiled. He came over and sat down. "Hey, didn't I see you on TV?" he asked Elizabeth.

"You sure did," Steven said proudly. "Meet my sister Elizabeth, the television star."

"I know your sister, Melissa," Elizabeth said. "We're in the same grade."

Andy smiled, but Elizabeth thought he looked uneasy. "You know Melissa, huh?"

Before Elizabeth could say anything else, Steven broke in. "Listen, Andy, I'm sorry about what happened at McRobert's last week."

"No problem," Andy said. "I've had jobs myself. I know about those types. Actually, I looked for you there this weekend. The manager was gone, and the girl behind the counter said you weren't there anymore."

"You were looking for me?" Steven asked, surprised.

"Yeah. I wanted to ask you about working there," Andy said. "I sort of need a job. I thought maybe you could put in a word for me."

Steven shook his head. "Believe me, a word from me wouldn't do you any good. Besides, it's a crummy place to work."

Andy shifted uncomfortably. "Yeah, well—a job's a job, right?" Andy stood up to leave. "If you hear of anything, let me know, OK?"

"Will do," Steven promised.

"Tell Melissa hi," Elizabeth said.

For just a second, Elizabeth could have sworn she saw that uneasy look again. But it was gone immediately. "I'll do that," he said, but Elizabeth couldn't help worrying that something was wrong with Andy McCormick and his sister, Melissa.

What's happened to Melissa and Andy? Find out in Sweet Valley Twins and Friends #58, **ELIZABETH AND THE ORPHANS.**

SWEET VALLEY TWINS™

Join Jessica and Elizabeth for
big adventure in exciting
SWEET VALLEY TWINS SUPER EDITIONS
and **SWEET VALLEY TWINS CHILLERS.**

☐ **#1: CLASS TRIP**   15588-1/$3.50
☐ **#2: HOLIDAY MISCHIEF**   15641-1/$3.50
☐ **#3: THE BIG CAMP SECRET**   15707-8/$3.50
☐ **#4: THE UNICORNS GO HAWAIIAN**   15948-8/$3.50
☐ **SWEET VALLEY TWINS SUPER SUMMER**
  FUN BOOK by Laurie Pascal Wenk   15816-3/$3.50

Elizabeth shares her favorite summer projects &
Jessica gives you pointers on parties. Plus:
fashion tips, space to record your favorite
summer activities, quizzes, puzzles, a summer
calendar, photo album, scrapbook, address book
& more!

CHILLERS

☐ **#1: THE CHRISTMAS GHOST**   15767-1/$3.50
☐ **#2: THE GHOST IN THE GRAVEYARD**

                                 15801-5/$3.50

☐ **#3: THE CARNIVAL GHOST**   15859-7/$2.95

The most exciting story ever in Sweet Valley history

FRANCINE PASCAL'S
SWEET VALLEY Saga

THE SWEET VALLEY SAGA tells the incredible story of the lives and times of five generations of brave and beautiful young women who were Jessica and Elizabeth's ancestors. Their story is the story of America: from the danger of the pioneering days to the glamour of the roaring nineties, the sacrifice and romance of World War II to the rebelliousness of the Sixties, right up to the present-day Sweet Valley. A dazzling novel of unforgettable lives and love both lost and won, THE SWEET VALLEY SAGA is Francine Pascal's most memorable, exciting, and wonderful Sweet Valley book ever.

BANTAM
NEW YORK • TORONTO • LONDON • SYDNEY • AUCKLAND

☐	27567-4	DOUBLE LOVE #1	$2.95
☐	27578-X	SECRETS #2	$2.99
☐	27669-7	PLAYING WITH FIRE #3	$2.99
☐	27493-7	POWER PLAY #4	$2.99
☐	27568-2	ALL NIGHT LONG #5	$2.99
☐	27741-3	DANGEROUS LOVE #6	$2.99
☐	27672-7	DEAR SISTER #7	$2.99
☐	27569-0	HEARTBREAKER #8	$2.99
☐	27878-9	RACING HEARTS #9	$2.99
☐	27668-9	WRONG KIND OF GIRL #10	$2.95
☐	27941-6	TOO GOOD TO BE TRUE #11	$2.99
☐	27755-3	WHEN LOVE DIES #12	$2.95
☐	27877-0	KIDNAPPED #13	$2.99
☐	27939-4	DECEPTIONS #14	$2.95
☐	27940-5	PROMISES #15	$3.25
☐	27431-7	RAGS TO RICHES #16	$2.95
☐	27931-9	LOVE LETTERS #17	$2.95
☐	27444-9	HEAD OVER HEELS #18	$2.95
☐	27589-5	SHOWDOWN #19	$2.95
☐	27454-6	CRASH LANDING! #20	$2.99
☐	27566-6	RUNAWAY #21	$2.99
☐	27952-1	TOO MUCH IN LOVE #22	$2.99
☐	27951-3	SAY GOODBYE #23	$2.99
☐	27492-9	MEMORIES #24	$2.99
☐	27944-9	NOWHERE TO RUN #25	$2.99
☐	27670-0	HOSTAGE #26	$2.95
☐	27885-1	LOVESTRUCK #27	$2.99
☐	28087-2	ALONE IN THE CROWD #28	$2.99

Buy them at your local bookstore or use this page to order.

Bantam Books, Dept. SVH, 2451 South Wolf Road, Des Plaines, IL 60018

Please send me the items I have checked above. I am enclosing $_____
(please add $2.50 to cover postage and handling). Send check or money
order, no cash or C.O.D.s please.

Mr/Ms _____

Address _____

City/State _____ Zip _____

SVH–3/92

Please allow four to six weeks for delivery.
Prices and availability subject to change without notice.